Donna Parker

On Her Own

By
MARCIA MARTIN

With illustrations by
SARI

WHITMAN PUBLISHING COMPANY
RACINE, WISCONSIN

Copyright, © MCMLVII, by
WHITMAN PUBLISHING COMPANY
PRINTED IN U.S.A

All names, characters, and events in this story
are entirely fictitious.

Contents

1. A Question 9
2. An Answer 25
3. Miss Dengrove Appears 40
4. Crooak! 53
5. This Is Living! 69
6. Problems 87
7. Five Dollars 98
8. Committees and Phone Calls 109
9. Suspicions 125
10. Mrs. Cunningham 145
11. More Money 167
12. The Dean's Office 183
13. The Party 200
14. Jimmy 214
15. Modern Methods 224
16. Flowers and Dresses 240
17. The Dance 253
18. Home Again 266

CHAPTER 1 — *A Question*

Donna Parker, her coat flying, ran lightly up the four cement steps and paused on her front porch. Shifting her school books to her left arm, she turned the knob of the heavy, old-fashioned front door, and then drew back. Should she ask now?

The warm sun touched Donna's face, and made her naturally rosy cheeks even rosier. She took a deep breath and drew in the scent of freshly turned earth, of new buds, of the promise of spring. It really was a beautiful day!

Her courage renewed, she flung open the door, laid her books on the hall table, and without even stopping to take off her coat, walked quickly to the end of the short hall and into the kitchen. As she had hoped, her mother was just beginning preparations for dinner.

"That you, Cooky?" Mrs. Parker asked, not turning

around from the sink. "I was just wondering what was keeping you. You didn't have to stay after school, did you?"

"Oh, no, Mommy," Donna answered quickly. "I was just talking to the girls—you know, Anne Franklin and Joyce Davenport and Mary Jefferson and Karen—"

"And Ricky West," added her mother, stooping to get some potatoes from the bin.

"Of course, Ricky too." Donna paused a moment as she pictured her best friend, whose red hair and lightly freckled face were in such contrast to her own dark hair and rosy complexion. It was true that Ricky was a dreamer, and was always dramatizing situations, but she did have some awfully good ideas, too, like—

"But you haven't even taken off your coat yet," said Mrs. Parker in a surprised tone, as she turned around and actually looked at her daughter.

"I know, Mommy," Donna mumbled, "but you see..." and she drew a deep breath.

"Now what?" asked her mother, hands on hips. "Donna, what are you up to now? That expression on your face means just one thing—trouble!" But from the indulgent look on Mrs. Parker's face, Donna knew she wasn't angry.

"Well," Donna took a deep breath, "we were all talking

about how dull life has been since our trip to New York, and somebody had a wonderful idea. How about all of us girls going on a camping trip next weekend?"

"A camping trip?" Now it was Mrs. Parker's turn to be perplexed. "But it's only March, Donna. I know today is almost like spring, but there might even be snow by next weekend. And where would you go, and what would you do?"

"Oh, Mommy, it would be wonderful. We'd hike someplace, maybe to the State Park, and we'd take knapsacks and sleeping bags, so we could cook out and sleep out, and we'd be back by Sunday night."

Mrs. Parker turned back to the sink. "I never heard of such nonsense, Donna. First, as I told you, it's much too early in the year for any such activity. The weather is still too treacherous. As for cooking out, I know the kind of meals you girls would have. Between the weather, and the thought of you building fires and not getting proper meals and sleeping on the ground, I'd worry every minute."

There was a moment's pause, and Mrs. Parker continued, "Would any of the mothers go with you?"

Donna looked up from her shoes, which seemed to be holding her attention. "But, Mommy, that's just the point.

We want to get away from mothers and be by ourselves. Goodness, we're not babies any more. We'd only be gone two days. What could possibly happen?"

"I know you're not a baby, Donna," her mother answered, trying to keep her tone gentle. "But you're still not old enough to go off for a weekend by yourself, unchaperoned, where goodness knows how many things can go wrong."

"But, Mommy," Donna remonstrated, "it couldn't possibly be cold next week. Why, you can smell spring in the air, and the sun is so lovely and warm. And I help you cook dinner at home; I don't know why I can't do it in the Park as well. I promise we'll have well-balanced meals—"

Mrs. Parker held up a warning hand. "Now, Donna, that's enough. I gave you my answer."

"It's not fair," said Donna sulkily. "All the other girls will go and I'll be left home. I don't know why you insist on treating me like a baby." She looked at her mother accusingly. "You just don't want me to have a good time. I can't ever do anything to enjoy myself!" Sobs began to shake her voice. "Only work, work, work!"

She flounced over to the kitchen table, seated herself

heavily on a chair and laid her head in her arms. "Everyone else can have fun, but I can't ever do anything. It's just not fair," she wailed.

"That will be enough, Donna," said Mrs. Parker coldly. "Certainly a performance like this will do nothing to convince me that you're grown-up. Now will you kindly take off your coat, and begin on your homework so you can get to bed at a reasonable hour?"

Donna lifted her head from the table and wiped her tearstained face with a tissue from her coat pocket. Slowly she gathered her books, and dragged her feet into the hall, sniffing as she went.

"I'll have to call Ricky and tell her," she thought sadly. Then, with a flood of resentment, "But I won't use the phone in the kitchen while she's in there. I can't even have any privacy," she thought bitterly. "Some girls have their own telephones, or at least an extension in their own rooms where the whole family doesn't listen to every word they say. But not little Donna, oh, no!" All her injustices seemed to crowd in upon her. Life was so difficult!

"I promised to take these cookies over to Mrs. Wood's for the P.T.A. meeting tomorrow, Donna," said Mrs. Parker as Donna was closing the closet door in the front hall. "Will you keep an eye on the potatoes? I'll only be gone a few minutes."

"As though nothing at all had happened," thought Donna. "But I can call Ricky now, at least," and she raced into the kitchen.

She dialed the number quickly and waited impatiently while the bell rang at the opposite end.

"Hello," said a young girl's voice.

"Oh, it's you, Rick," Donna said in relief. "Listen, I've got to talk fast. *She's* going to be back in a few minutes."

"Oh, Donna," Ricky West said sadly. "You mean you can't go?"

Donna gasped. "How did you know? I didn't say a word."

"When you call your mother *she,* in that tone of voice, you don't have to say anything," Ricky replied ominously. "I just know."

"Isn't it dreadful?" wailed Donna. "I guess she thinks we'll set ourselves on fire or something. She even said the weather might be freezing, or it might snow. Imagine, when everyone knows that it's March already, and spring is practically here. It's just an excuse, I know."

"Well, if it's any consolation, Don, I can't go either."

"You can't?" Donna didn't know whether to be sorry for her friend's sake, or happy for her own. "Mothers certainly are a problem, aren't they?"

The two girls were silent for a moment. Then Donna heaved a deep sigh. "Someday we'll surprise them and show them that we really are grown-up."

There was the sound of a door closing, and the dark-haired girl jumped. "Here she comes now, Rick," she said in a low voice. "I'd better go." And she quickly put down the receiver.

"You haven't started your lessons yet, Donna?" asked Mrs. Parker, as she came back into the kitchen and reached for her apron.

"No, I was"—Donna looked around for an excuse—"I was just looking at the potatoes," and she lifted the lid of the steaming pot.

"Well, while you're here you may as well give your bird its food and water. And be sure you change the paper at the bottom of the cage. It's a disgrace!"

"Yes, Mother," said Donna meekly, but inside she was still fuming. *My goodness, does she have to tell me every little thing?*

Armed with several sheets of newspaper, a box of birdseed, and a little jar of water, she went into the small room adjoining the kitchen. It was still called the "back porch," although it had been enclosed ever since Donna could remember.

She put the newspaper, water, and birdseed on a small table, and went over to the far end of the room. There, on an arrangement of wooden boxes, stood a bird cage about twice the size of a canary's cage, and in it sat a large white bird.

The bird had not arrived in its present cage. Donna's father had brought it home one night, a large package wrapped in a dark blue towel.

"Whatever is that?" Donna's mother had asked, and Mr. Parker had smiled sheepishly.

"It's a gift for Donna. Now don't get excited," he added hastily as he saw the reproving look on Mrs. Parker's face. "I know you don't like animals in the house, Grace, and I promised I wouldn't bring home any more dogs or cats, but this was given to me."

Mrs. Parker's face was blank. She was obviously withholding judgment until she saw what was under the blue towel.

"A customer came in with it today," continued Mr. Parker, "and said he had used it in a display, and now he didn't know what to do with it. So I offered to take it, and he was really very grateful. Of course, if you don't want to keep it, I can give it back. But I know how crazy Donna is about animals, and she's never had anything except a few goldfish." And he pulled the towel off the cage, exposing a pure white dove.

"Oh, how beautiful!" Donna cried. "It looks like the doves on Christmas cards. Is that what it is, really and truly, Daddy—a dove?"

"A dove!" said Mrs. Parker, in a tone which said better than words that this was really beyond belief. "Of all things, a dove!"

"Hey, that's pretty neat!" exclaimed Jimmy, Donna's eight-year-old brother. "Does it eat worms and bugs and things?"

"Jimmy!" Donna warned. How did he always manage to say exactly the wrong thing?

"No," Mr. Parker answered quickly. "Doves are part of the pigeon family, and they eat birdseed, not bugs. They're very quiet birds, too, Grace, and I'm sure this one wouldn't bother you at all."

"Oh, I'd take such good care of it, Mommy," Donna

chimed in quickly. "Oh, thank you, Daddy, thank you. It's a wonderful present."

Mrs. Parker shrugged her shoulders. "Well, I can't say I like the idea, but all right . . . ." The rest of the sentence had been smothered in a quick hug from her daughter.

Donna had been disappointed at not being able to keep the bird in her room, but Mrs. Parker had been firm about it. And when the man at the pet store had told Donna that a dove needed a "flight cage," and she had spent her few hard-earned dollars for the largest one he had and had lugged it home, the very size of the cage necessitated it being put on the back porch.

All this went quickly through Donna's mind as she opened the door of the cage and gently gathered the bird into her cupped hands. It still seemed like a half-wild thing when freed, and she held it carefully while she went back to close the door to the kitchen.

"Goodness, if it ever got in there and started to fly around, I'll bet Mother would have a stroke," Donna thought, brushing the soft white feathers tenderly, and putting the bird down on the small table. Her eyes welled up with tears again.

"Why can't I have a mother who lets me have pets?"

she murmured. "When I'm a mother, my children will be allowed to have any animals they want, and I'll let them sleep in the same rooms with them, too."

She filled the little water dish and shook some fresh birdseed into the container suspended from the side of the cage. Then, wrinkling her nose, she gathered together the newspapers that lined the bottom of the cage.

"Ugh," she shuddered, wadding the papers into a tight roll. "Doves look so clean and white and beautiful. I never knew they could make such a mess." Deftly she put the clean newspapers down. Then she took out the perch on which the dove sat, and with a special wire brush she scrubbed it until it looked clean and new.

"Now you go back in your nice clean house," said Donna cheerfully as she went over to the table on which she had placed the bird.

But where was he? Donna looked around, startled, for she had heard no whirring of wings. Not on the window sill, not in the laundry basket, nowhere on the floor. The door to the kitchen was still closed, and the door to the back yard had not been opened at all. And then, from under the cage, in the collection of boxes on which it rested, she heard a fluttering sound. With a gasp of relief she ran to the cage. There was the bird, wedged between two boxes.

"Oh, you silly thing," she cooed, "how did you ever get down here? There, now you're out. And back you go." With one motion the dove was back in the cage and the wire door closed.

"Now you can't get out," she warned, backing toward the kitchen door. "But I'll be here again soon."

"Well, finally," said Mrs. Parker as Donna continued to back into the kitchen. "It's dreadfully late. I think I hear Daddy already, and you haven't started setting the table."

"Yes, Mother," said Donna with no trace of friendliness in her voice, and not looking to see the sharp glance her mother sent her.

She was busy arranging napkins when Mr. Parker strode in, hung up his coat, and went into the kitchen.

"Hi, honey," he said, as he put his arms around Mrs. Parker's waist. "Have a good day?" Then, catching a glimpse of Donna in the dining room, he called, "Hi, sweetie. What's new? Where's Jimmy?"

"Well," said Mrs. Parker, drying her hands and taking off her apron. "You sound cheerful, Sam. What's made you so happy?"

Mr. Parker looked at her. "Now, can't a man be glad

to come home to a lovely family like this?"

"Oh, goodness," thought Donna. "Wait'll Mommy tells him about the fight we had. He won't think we're such a lovely family."

"Oh, Sam," his wife laughed. "After all these years, do you think I can't tell when you have something special on your mind?"

Mr. Parker sat down at the kitchen table and motioned to his wife to join him. "Just for a minute, honey," he said, as Mrs. Parker looked at the pots bubbling on the stove.

"I got a call from Warren Holmes today. Remember, he was here one night last year and we had that long talk about distribution problems abroad?"

Donna, putting salt shakers on the table, nodded to herself. Mr. Holmes had been a fascinating man. She didn't know much about him, though, except that he spent much of his time traveling abroad on business.

"Well, he said he's never forgotten what I told him about my ideas. You know, how to make it easier for foreign countries, which don't know much about American methods, to get things from their factories to places where people can buy the goods. Not every country has department stores and supermarkets, you know."

Mrs. Parker merely nodded.

"He's just come back from a trip to the Far East, and he wondered if I could take some time off from the office." Mr. Parker got up and started to walk around the table, as though that would make it easier for him to find the proper words.

"You see," he continued, "his company would like me to act as consultant for a couple of months." He paused.

"But where?" asked Mrs. Parker, puzzled.

"Where?" Mr. Parker stopped. "Oh, I thought I told you. They want me to go to India."

Donna gasped. India! It was like going to the moon.

"It's such an opportunity!" Mr. Parker continued. "Just think—the Taj Mahal, and elephants, and ivory . . . . It's a part of the world I thought we'd never get to see."

"We?" Mrs. Parker caught the word immediately. "You mean you wouldn't go alone?"

"Of course I wouldn't. How would I feel, seeing all those wonderful things and not being able to share them? And Warren Holmes agreed. He always takes his family with him."

Donna stood perfectly still for a second. India! That wonderful, romantic country halfway around the world.

And her dear wonderful father had said he wouldn't go alone.

She flew into the kitchen and flung her arms around her father's neck.

"Oh, Daddy! Daddy dear!" she cried. "I'd love to go to India with you!"

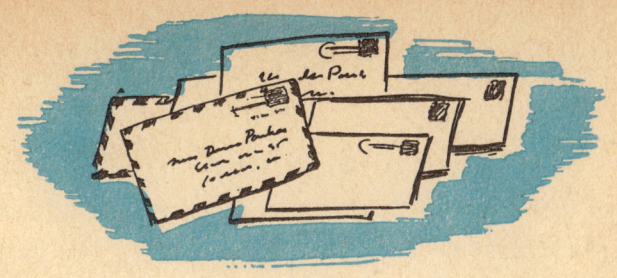

CHAPTER 2　　　　　　　　　　*An Answer*

Mr. Parker gently disengaged his daughter's arms from around his neck.

"Why, Donna, I don't know whether the invitation includes you or not."

"But, Daddy," and Donna's dark eyes widened, "you said you wanted us to see the Taj Mahal and all those other things."

Mr. Parker exchanged a glance with his wife. Then he rubbed the back of his neck. "I meant I didn't want to go without Mother. Of course," he added hastily, "I think it would be wonderful if you and Jimmy could come, too. I mean if we could make arrangements about school and all those other things."

"Oh, school! Pooh!" said Donna. "I'd learn a lot more on the trip than I ever would in any old school. Anyhow,

Easter vacation is coming soon, and school will be closed for a week."

Mrs. Parker stood up from the kitchen table. "Now let's just keep our feet on the ground for a while. First, Sam, you'd better find out more details—how long they'd want you to be gone, and what Mr. Holmes would do about paying expenses, and whether or not you can leave the office. And then we'll worry about the children."

"Worry?" asked a squeaky voice, as the door between the kitchen and the back porch was flung open and Jimmy appeared. "You don't have to worry about me."

"Jimmy!" exclaimed Mrs. Parker. "Did you come in the back way again, after all I've told you?"

"Aw, Ma, the back way is much shorter. And I only climbed over one fence. See, my dungarees aren't tore at all."

"Aren't *torn*," corrected Donna under her breath. Why couldn't an eight-year-old boy speak correct English?

"Anyhow," he mumbled through a mouthful of cookies which he had managed to stuff into his mouth before his mother could stop him, "why're ya worrying?"

Mr. Parker smiled. "We're not really, Jimmy. We were just wondering what arrangements we'd make for you if we go away. A friend of mine would like me to go to India."

"India!" Jimmy's hand stopped halfway to the cooky box. "Say, could you bring back a real stuffed tiger head, or maybe an elephant tusk?"

Mr. Parker laughed. "Mr. Holmes wants me to go on business, not on a hunting expedition, Jimmy."

"But wouldn't you want to go too, Jimmy?" Donna asked, hoping to make an ally of her brother.

"Who, me? Sure. I'd love to. But I couldn't leave the guys. We're just gettin' the team together, and maybe we'll be able to begin practice next week."

"What is it now, Jimmy?" Mrs. Parker laughed. "Football, basketball, or baseball?"

"Aw, Ma." Jimmy's disgust was obvious. "You know that in the spring you play baseball. Football's in the fall, an' basketball's in the winter."

"I know I'll never work up the enthusiasm you have for any of them, James, my boy," replied Mrs. Parker. "And since dinner is ready to be served, I suggest you stop filling up on cookies. Not that it seems to interfere with your appetite. Really, I don't know where you put it all."

"He's a growing, active boy, Grace," said Mr. Parker,

as Jimmy went off to wash his hands.

"But what about *India?*" asked Donna, who was disturbed that the conversation had gotten so far away from the subject that most interested her.

"Now, honey," said Mr. Parker, patting her shiny dark hair. "I'll get the answers to all Mother's questions, and tomorrow night we'll discuss the matter again."

Donna realized that the subject was closed. But she could not stop her thoughts from racing. Throughout dinner and the evening, all the time she was doing her homework, getting ready for bed, and even as she was dropping off to sleep, her mind seemed to hum a little tune: *Maybe I'll go to India! Maybe I'll go to India!*

She awoke the next morning and the tune sprang immediately into her mind. She could hardly wait until Ricky rang the doorbell, so that she could talk to her on the way to school.

"Oh, it's so exciting!" cried Ricky when she had listened to Donna's story. "Maybe you'll meet a prince, or a maharajah, and he'll shower you with diamonds and rubies, and give huge banquets for you where you eat peacocks' tongues and all kinds of things."

Donna giggled. "Oh, Ricky. Peacocks' tongues! And

rubies! Where do you get those crazy ideas?" Then her tone became sober. "It's not at all definite that I'm going, you know. In fact, it's not even definite that Daddy's going. He said he'd know more about it tonight."

"Promise that the minute you know, you'll tell me," said Ricky earnestly. "You know you always have exciting things happen to you. But this is the most exciting of all! It makes the camping trip look like real kid stuff."

"Camping trip!" exclaimed Donna. "Why, do you know, Ricky, I completely forgot all about it! And of course I'll call you as soon as I find out."

Several times during the school day Donna caught herself dreaming. Visions of marble palaces and turbaned princes rose before her, and mysterious dark-eyed women, draped in graceful saris, served exotic foods to her.

She rushed home immediately after school, and began the long impatient wait for Mr. Parker to arrive.

Much to Donna's disappointment, neither of her parents would discuss the matter until after dinner. For once Donna was anxious to clear the table and do the dishes.

"Now!" she said, as she looked around to see that the last pots had been put away, the kitchen counter tops wiped, and the floor swept. "Now can we talk about the trip?"

"Let's all go into the living room and sit down," said Mr. Parker. "Then we can discuss the whole matter. You too, Jimmy," he added as he noticed his son edging out the kitchen door.

"Yes, sir," Jimmy answered despondently, thrusting his fists into his pockets. They all knew that Jimmy disliked family conferences intensely, for much as he enjoyed being treated like an adult, he found it extremely difficult to sit still long enough to listen to what was being said.

Everyone trooped into the living room and sat down—the comfortable lounge chair known as the Daddy chair being reserved, of course, for Donna's father. Then there was a moment's silence and everyone looked expectantly at Mr. Parker. He cleared his throat.

"Well, I called Mr. Holmes again today and went over everything with him. And frankly," he looked at Mrs. Parker as he said this, "things seem even more exciting than they first appeared. I'd have to spend at least a month in India, but with good plane connections the trip each way wouldn't take much more than two days. Six weeks would be ample to allow for the whole thing."

"Two days to go halfway around the world. Wow!" said Jimmy. "That's really making time."

"The problem," Mr. Parker continued, "is that with the clock being pushed back so fast, it's very difficult on one's body to make the adjustment, so Mr. Holmes suggested that we stop over for two or three days in Europe on the way there or back. He said most of their people stay in London, Paris, or Rome, all of which have good connections to India. We could do a little sight-seeing, maybe a little shopping, and get used to the time change more gradually. What do you think of that?"

Donna watched her father. He looked as though he had just handed her mother a diamond necklace which he knew would overwhelm her, but was afraid he would be told that his wife no longer liked diamonds.

"But she's really excited!" thought Donna. "I've never seen her eyes sparkle so."

"Really, Sam?" Mrs. Parker was saying. "Paris or Rome or London! How wonderful! That would make up for any problems we'd have to face in India. Quite frankly, I took several books on India out of the library today, and even though it sounds like a wonderful, glamorous place, there are drawbacks. What kind of places would we visit? Would we stay in the big cities, or the villages, or what?"

"I was just coming to that," said Mr. Parker. "We'd go

from Europe straight on to India, to New Delhi, which is the capital. But most of our time would be spent in South India, in Madras, which is quite a large city, and in smaller cities all the way down to the very tip of the country."

"Oh, Daddy!" squealed Donna. "We studied about that last year. It's just like the Amazon Valley in Brazil, it's so tropical. And that's where all the wonderful spices and silks of India come from. Oh, wait till I tell the girls!"

Jimmy had begun to fidget. "Gee, this sounds like a geography lesson," he complained. "I get enough of that at school every day. Can't I go now?"

"Just a few more minutes, now, Jimmy," said Mr. Parker sternly. "It won't hurt you to listen." Then he turned to his wife again. "We'd have to work awfully quickly, to get all our passports and visas from the State Department. And then we'd have to crowd in all our shots."

"Shots?" asked Jimmy. "What kind of shots?"

"Injections, silly," said Donna. "You can't go abroad without having a vaccination. Well, I have mine."

"Me, too," said Jimmy, rolling up his sleeve and inspecting a tiny scarred place on his arm, then showing it proudly to all the family. "Yep, there it *is*!"

Again Mr. Parker looked uncomfortable. "Donna, I'm

afraid it's a lot more than just a vaccination. We sometimes forget how advanced the United States is, compared with some other countries in the world. And India doesn't have even the most elementary sanitary standards in some places. So, besides the vaccination—and it would mean a new one —Mr. Holmes gave me a long list of other things." He pulled a slip of paper from his pocket and read off, "Typhoid and paratyphoid, typhus, tetanus, whooping cough, diphtheria, cholera, and yellow fever. And then," looking up from the paper, "medicine against malaria and dysentery all the time we're over there."

"Oh-oh!" said Jimmy. "Not for me, thanks. Anyhow, I can't leave my gang. So can I be excused now, please?" Mrs. Parker merely looked at him and he subsided.

Donna was quiet. She felt her mother and father both watching her intently. Then she took a deep breath, squared her shoulders, and said, "That's all right. If you can take all those injections, then I can too."

"But, Donna," said Mrs. Parker gently, "you get upset when the doctor merely pricks your finger to take a drop of blood. And you might really get sick from some of these, you know, honey. Some people have dreadful reactions."

"Well, I won't!" persisted Donna stubbornly. Mr. Parker

looked helplessly at his wife, then turned again to his daughter. "You really want to go very badly, don't you, dear?"

"Oh, yes, Daddy, so very, very much. I promise I'll be good." What was happening? What did these glances between her mother and father mean?

Mr. Parker got out of his chair and came over to sit beside Donna on the couch.

"Look, honey," he said gently. "I thought you'd understand. The trip will be very difficult. It will entail a great deal of flying, and you'd be exposed to all sorts of diseases in India. I really can't take the responsibility of worrying about you and still do a decent job for Mr. Holmes. Besides, you can't miss six weeks of junior high."

Donna withdrew her hand from her father's. "You—you mean I can't go? You won't let me?"

Mr. Parker nodded his head silently.

"You and Mother will go," and she tried hard to keep back the sobs, "and you'll leave me here alone with that—that—" She pointed to her brother, but words failed her.

"We'll make arrangements for you, somehow, honey."

"But you won't let me go!" She stood up and faced her parents accusingly.

"I'm sorry, dear, but we both think it best this way," replied Mr. Parker.

"Oh! Oh, you're both so *mean!*" she cried, and turning on her heel, rushed out of the room, up the stairs, and flung herself on her bed. Then the sobs overwhelmed her. Her shoulders heaved and she could feel the bedspread getting damp beneath her face. After all her hopes and dreams! And after she had told the girls and was becoming quite a celebrity.

And they didn't even have a good reason. That was parents for you! It was perfectly all right for them to go traveling all over the world! But when it came to letting her have some fun, too, and doing something really exciting, then they had a million excuses. Too dangerous—imagine! And missing school! Why, this trip would be very educational. They were just plain mean! She buried her head deeper into the pillow and sobbed.

There was a light tap at the door. "Who is it?" she asked, her voice muffled by the pillow.

The door opened softly, and Mr. Parker came in. He sat down on the edge of the bed.

"Turn around, Donna," he said gently. "I want to talk to you."

"I-I don't want to see you," she said bitterly. "There's nothing to s-say. I can't go. Th-that's all there is. B-But I don't have to be h-happy about it, do I?" She sniffed audibly.

"Honey, I'm terribly sorry to make you unhappy. Believe me, if I thought it were possible there's nothing I'd like better than to have you come with us. But, Donna, aside from all the things we just talked about, there's another reason why you can't come."

"Th-there is?" Donna half turned over so she could see her father out of one eye.

"Mr. Holmes said he would pay expenses and transportation for both your mother and me. But he can't pay your expenses. And do you know how much the fare is?"

"How much?" asked Donna suspiciously.

"It's a lot over a thousand dollars, even if we went the cheapest way possible. And that doesn't include hotel bills, or meals, or anything else. So we'd have to allow from fifteen hundred to two thousand dollars for your share of the trip."

"That much?" Donna sat up, wide-eyed. Then she fell back on the bed. "But that doesn't make me any happier. You and Mother will go, and who will take care of me?"

"Well, now," Mr. Parker said. "Mother just had a sug-

gestion. If you don't want to stay here with Jimmy—and I really don't know where we'd find someone to stay with you—then, how would you like to go to a boarding school?"

"A boarding school?" Donna felt that she was becoming an echo, repeating everything her father said. "You mean to *live* there?"

Mr. Parker nodded. "For the time we're gone. That is, if we can find a good one. How would that suit you?"

"Well, at least it would be better than staying here." She looked around her.

"We'll see what we can do." Mr. Parker tiptoed out, leaving Donna with a whole new train of thoughts.

Of course, she was still unhappy about not going to India. That would have been so glamorous. But then, a boarding school was better than nothing. Maybe she would make some wonderful new friends. Maybe, even, some of them would have older brothers who would be very anxious to meet her. "So you're my little sister's roommate!" She could hear the male voice, even if she couldn't see the face. "Why didn't she tell me you were so attractive?"

She took out her math book and settled herself at her desk. Actually, boarding school might be even better than going to India. She could still say, "My parents? Didn't you know? They're abroad. Oh, just Paris and Rome, and a month in India."

And she would be here, on her own. What she had been dreaming of for so long. After this, they would have to treat her like an adult. She would show them how mature and responsible a person she could be. Imagine, nobody to keep after her every minute, saying, "Donna, do your homework. Donna, clean the bird cage."

She stopped, her pencil poised in the air. Her dove! If she went to boarding school, what would she do with it? She'd have to find someone at school who would take it while she was gone. Ricky didn't like pets any more than Mrs. Parker did, but there must be someone else who would be glad to have a beautiful white dove.

Lying in bed later, she thought over all the things her father had said. Maybe he was right, after all. To fly all those thousands of miles! To be in a country that was so strange, so different. Her parents were really taking chances. Suppose something happened to them! Or suppose she didn't like the boarding school. Goodness, there were a lot of things to worry about.

CHAPTER 3   *Miss Dengrove Appears*

"Oh, Mommy," Donna said the next morning at breakfast. "I was so excited last night I could hardly sleep." She picked up her glass of orange juice. "Did you really mean what Daddy told me about boarding school?"

Mrs. Parker breathed a silent prayer of relief. Sometimes she felt that she would never know how her daughter's mind worked. Last night, listening to the sobs, she was sure that Donna would never forgive them for going away without her. Not that she could really blame her—if it weren't for all the complications, she would really love to have her daughter along.

But obviously there was no need to worry. Donna not only seemed to have gotten used to the idea, but she was almost as excited about going to boarding school as she had been about India.

"Do you know the names of any schools around here that you'd like me to call?" asked Mrs. Parker. "I'd want to be absolutely sure that you'd be well cared for while we're gone."

Donna thought for a moment, then shook her head. "Gee, Mommy, I can't think of any. Maybe Mr. Greer would know some."

"That's a good idea, Donna. A junior high school principal must have contact with other schools in the vicinity. I'll call him this morning."

"And I'll ask the girls at school whether they know of any."

A bell rang and Donna leaped up from the table. "Is that Ricky already? I didn't realize it was so late."

"My, Donna, you really are living in a dream world," laughed Mrs. Parker as the bell rang again. "That's the telephone, silly, not the doorbell."

Donna sank back as her mother lifted the receiver. "Babette? Oh, good morning. Is anything wrong? No, but whenever you call so early I think maybe Jimmy's gotten into some mischief again."

Babette Gray was the Parkers' next-door neighbor and the mother of Skipper, Jimmy's best friend. Donna, like her mother, had learned that together Skipper and Jimmy constantly got into scrapes. "One eight-year-old boy is enough," thought Donna, "but heaven protect me from two of them. I don't know how they ever get those crazy ideas—like mixing all the chemicals from their sets to make a 'magic potion,' and making such an odor that no one could walk into the basement for days."

But from the expression on Mrs. Parker's face, Donna could tell that no trouble was afoot.

"I guess she just wants to have a friendly conversation," thought Donna, gathering her books. "I'd better not wait for this to end; it can go on for hours."

She saw Ricky coming up the front steps, and the thought of boarding school rushed into her mind.

"Oh, Ricky," she cried, almost colliding with her friend, "wait'll I tell you what's happened now!"

"Even a trip to the moon wouldn't surprise me," said Ricky. "But seriously, Don, can you really go with your mother and father? I'll bet the answer's Yes, or you wouldn't look so happy."

Donna slowed her pace for a moment. It would have been fun to say that Ricky had guessed correctly, that she was really going to India. Then she tossed her head.

"Well, smarty, the answer is *not* Yes."

"Oh, Donna!" Ricky looked sympathetically at the dark-haired girl. "But why?"

"Well, I was beginning to think maybe it wasn't such a good idea after all. You know, I've never been in an airplane before, and I was a little scared of flying so far for my very first time."

"Pooh!" answered Ricky. "My father flies all the time. Why, he goes to California or Texas the way we go to school. It's all in a day's work for him."

"Well," said Donna, realizing that she wasn't being very convincing, "did I tell you about all the shots I'd have to get? And then I was thinking about the food—you know how fussy I am about what I eat. And I thought it just wouldn't be fair to my parents to have them worrying about me all the time."

"Oh, Donna," said Ricky. "You mean they won't let you go?"

Donna looked at the red-haired girl by her side with an expression of dismay. Apparently she hadn't fooled her a bit. And she didn't want anyone feeling sorry for her—that would only make her feel worse.

"But I don't understand," Ricky said in a perplexed tone.

"If you're not going, why did you look so happy?"

"Oh, Ricky," Donna giggled. "My mind wanders off so quickly I almost forgot. You see, Mother and Daddy said that when they go away I could go to boarding school! Wouldn't that be super?"

"Boarding school!" Ricky turned to Donna with new respect in her eyes. "A real boarding school, where they have pajama parties, and make fudge late at night on somebody's little cook stove that the headmistress doesn't know about, and you get invited to somebody's mansion for the holidays?" Ricky paused for breath.

"Wouldn't it be wonderful, Rick? Of course I'd have to study, too, and the girls might not like me at first. It wouldn't be all fun, I guess."

"Oh, you'd make some wonderful friends, Don." The red-haired girl looked troubled. "In fact, you might like some of them more than you like me."

Donna squeezed her companion's arm. "Now you're being silly, Rick. You know you'll always be my best friend. But we'd better hurry. There goes the first bell. Will you see if you can find out the names of some schools for me? Meet you after school!" And with a wave of her arm, Donna disappeared down the hall.

Lunch period was spent in discussing Donna's problem. All the girls thought the new plan was an excellent solution, but no one was able to give a single suggestion to Donna.

"I'll ask at home," said Mary Jefferson. "Maybe my mother or father knows of a nice place for you to stay." The other girls agreed to do the same thing.

"And I'll even let you take one of my white mice to keep you company," offered Anne Franklin.

"No, thanks," Donna shuddered. "I like most pets, but not mice. But, Anne, would you keep my dove while I'm gone? It's really not very much trouble."

"Gee, Donna, I'm not sure," Anne answered. "My parents say that if I bring one more animal into the house, they'll have to move out. But I'll see."

"Things certainly get complicated," Donna said to Ricky as they walked home after school. "I hope I don't have trouble finding a place to keep my dove. Though why I should be worrying about a little thing like that, I don't know. Nobody even knows of a single boarding school. Can you imagine that?"

"I heard about one," said Ricky. "But I don't think it's what you're looking for. It's called Maribel Hall, and all the girls are awfully rich and stuck-up. They even have their own horses."

"If I had a fairy godmother, maybe she'd turn one of Anne's white mice into a horse for me."

"And then suppose you were out riding at midnight," Ricky giggled. "All of a sudden, there you'd be, riding a white mouse—or trying to. Oh, I'd love to see the faces of the other girls when they saw you!"

"Maybe Mother has found a school," suggested Donna, becoming serious. "Mr. Greer ought to know of some."

But here, too, Donna was doomed to disappointment.

"The only school Mr. Greer could recommend," said Mrs. Parker after Donna had told her the events of the day, "was Maribel Hall, and—"

"I know, Mommy, I wouldn't even want to go there."

"But he did say he'd try to find something in his school directory," added Mrs. Parker.

Donna picked up her books and started for her bedroom.

"Just a minute, Donna. There's something else I'd like to talk to you about. Mrs. Gray called early this morning, you know."

Donna nodded and waited. What could Mrs. Gray have said that concerned her?

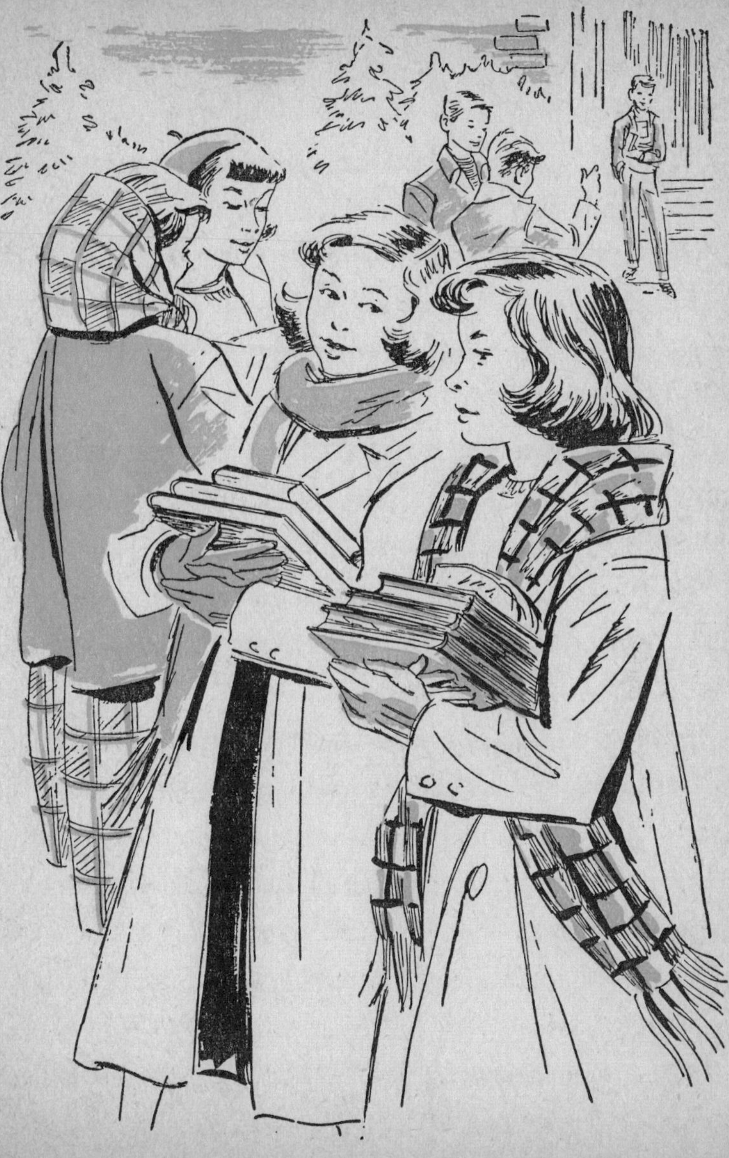

"Last night," Mrs. Parker went on, "she had Susan's new teacher to dinner." Susan was Skipper's six-year-old sister. "Her name is Miss Dengrove, and Mrs. Gray said that she's a lovely, attractive, sweet young woman."

"Oh, dear," thought Donna. "Now what's coming?"

"But she's very unhappy," continued her mother. "She couldn't find a single small apartment in Summerfield, so she's living in a rented room. She has to go out for all her meals, even breakfast. She was so happy to sit in a real living room after being cooped up in her little room for so long, that Babette said it made her feel good just to look at her."

"But what can we do, Mommy—have Miss Dengrove to dinner here?" Why was her mother discussing it with her?

"Now don't get upset, Donna, till you've heard me through. Since we're having trouble about the boarding school, and that wouldn't solve my problem about Jimmy anyhow, how would you feel about my asking Miss Dengrove to stay here?"

She held up a warning hand as Donna opened her mouth to speak.

"She could use our bedroom for the six weeks we're gone, and she'd be here to keep an eye on you and Jimmy. Susan seems very fond of her, and you might be, too. She might not want to stay here, of course. On the other hand, if the plan were agreeable to her I would want your consent, and Jimmy's, too."

Donna frowned. "And if we didn't like her, would you go ahead about the boarding school?"

"Of course," agreed her mother.

"Well, all right," said Donna hesitantly. "I guess there'd be no harm done. When would we meet her?"

"Suppose I ask her to dinner tomorrow night. I'll just make it a simple dinner invitation until I see how you feel about her. If we don't settle this soon, I'll have to tell Daddy that I just won't be able to go with him. There are only a few weeks left, you know."

It wasn't fair, thought Donna as she plumped down on her bed. Did all mothers put their daughters in predicaments like this? She had given in very gracefully about not going to India, she thought, completely forgetting about the scene and the tears of the night before. But if they couldn't find a suitable boarding school, and she said she didn't like Miss Dengrove, then her mother would stay home. And how could she take the responsibility for that? How would she feel, knowing that because of her,

her mother had missed the only chance she might ever have to go abroad?

This Miss Dengrove might be young, but she'd bet she was the mean, tight-lipped kind who would never let anybody have any fun. And she would probably nag all the time about homework and hanging up clothes, and turn up her nose at the dove. Why, oh, why did this sort of thing always happen to her? The one time in her life when she thought she'd be able to enjoy herself!

When Donna opened the front door the next evening, however, in answer to Miss Dengrove's ring, she immediately revised her opinion of the teacher.

"Why, she's really cute!" she thought. "And what a pretty dress she's wearing! Gee, I wonder if Mommy could make me one like that."

When Miss Dengrove offered to show Donna how to put wire in her petticoats, to make hoop skirts out of them, Donna was thrilled. And when the white dove was shown, and Miss Dengrove stroked its feathers tenderly and cooed to it, Donna lost her heart completely.

"She treats me like an equal, not a child," she decided joyfully. "And she doesn't think I'm silly or irresponsible.

If she stayed with us, it would be like having one of my own friends. I'll bet we could really have fun. I wonder what she'll think of Jimmy. I wouldn't blame her if she didn't want to stay here with that little monster."

But Donna was due for another surprise. For when Jimmy came in from playing, he took one look at Miss Dengrove and without a word disappeared upstairs. In a few minutes he was back again attired in a clean shirt, and with his hair slicked down and dripping wet.

Neither Miss Dengrove nor Mrs. Parker could restrain a smile as the child strode boldly up to the teacher, held out a not too clean hand and said, "Hi. I'm Jimmy."

"How do you do, Jimmy. I've seen you at school, and I've certainly admired the way you can throw a ball. You might even join a major league team some day if you keep up the good work." The teacher smiled warmly.

"But I can't bat so good," said Jimmy with delight, but modestly, obviously deciding that with such an appreciative audience there was no need to swagger.

"Your ears are dirty," said Donna in a stage whisper. Jimmy, however, was so enthralled with the guest that he either didn't hear, or didn't feel it was in keeping with his new character to respond to his sister in his usual manner.

When Mr. Parker appeared a few minutes later, Mrs. Parker introduced him and then asked Donna to help her in the kitchen.

"Oh, Mommy, she's not at all like I thought," said Donna in a confidential tone. "She's—why, she's not much older than I am."

"She seems like a lovely person," Mrs. Parker agreed, "and she's responsible, I'm sure. She'd have to be, to teach school. The principal and everyone else I've spoken to think very highly of her. Jimmy certainly seemed smitten, didn't he?"

"I've never seen him act so gentlemanly, Mommy," said Donna, putting the mashed potatoes in a bowl. "I think maybe it would be fun to have Miss Dengrove stay here with us. We could do lots of things together. And I wouldn't have to leave my friends, or miss school."

There was a moment's silence as Mrs. Parker took the hot rolls out of the oven.

"But do you think she'd agree to come for six weeks?" asked Donna. "I guess it wouldn't be much fun for her."

"I don't know, Donna. We'll have to wait and see."

CHAPTER 4 — *Crooak!*

"Ricky, Ricky, guess what!" Donna flew down the steps to meet her friend. Luckily it was a Saturday and they could spend more time together than the few minutes it took to walk to and from school.

"I don't know why you couldn't tell me on the phone, Donna," Ricky complained. "I've been absolutely dying of suspense."

"First thing this morning, Miss Dengrove called. She said she'd been thinking over the matter and—"

"Tell me! Was her answer Yes or No? Get to the point, Don."

"If you give me a chance, I will. Come up to my bedroom. We can talk better there than down here in the living room."

Ricky practically pushed her friend up the steps and

put her down on the bed. Then she sat down, too, and tucked her legs underneath her. "Now spill it!"

Donna sat cross-legged and picked up the large stuffed animal that lay on her pillow. "She said she thought our house was so comfortable, and we were two such well-behaved children." Donna grimaced. "Imagine thinking Jimmy is well-behaved! Although I will admit he's been a perfect little gentleman around her. Well, that won't last long, I'll bet."

"Then she'll come and stay with you?"

Donna nodded.

"For the whole six weeks, Donna? Even during the Easter vacation, when there is no school?"

Again the dark-haired girl nodded. "She said she had no place special to go then, anyhow. Oh, Ricky, this'll be such fun. It'll be almost like having the house to ourselves. Miss Dengrove—she said I could call her Marjorie, but it feels funny to call a teacher by her first name—she was telling me all about the parties she used to have when she was my age. She has wonderful ideas, Rick. Did you know about hanging up lumps of sugar for a sweet-sixteen party? You tie them into something that looks like a bunch of grapes and hang them up like mistletoe."

"Mistletoe's for Christmas," protested Ricky.

"I know. But the purpose is the same." Donna giggled. "Every time a boy catches you standing under the sugar he has to kiss you. When my mother and father heard her talking about kissing, I think they were a little shocked. But she knows what it's like to be our age, and she doesn't think we're babies, like our parents do. Oh, Ricky, we'll have some wonderful times. I'm so glad we couldn't find a boarding school right away."

"So'm I," agreed Ricky. "I didn't want to say anything, but I really would have missed you if you had gone to boarding school or to India. Say, when are your parents leaving?"

"In just a couple of weeks. Frankly, I don't know how they'll ever get everything done on time. Mother's hardly ever home any more. Yesterday she and Daddy had to get their pictures taken for their passports, and now she's at the doctor's getting some more shots. You ought to see all the things she bought, too. She says she feels like a bride getting her trousseau together. Come in her room and I'll show you."

"Wow!" exclaimed Ricky, as Donna led her into the front bedroom. "It looks as though they're going to be gone a year, not a few weeks. Look at those piles of things."

"That's my favorite," said Donna, pointing to a blue silk print dress hanging from the closet door. "It doesn't look like much on the hanger, but when Mommy puts it on it has a real low-cut neck, and her shoulders show, too. She actually looks glamorous, Rick." Donna looked at the dress in admiration. Imagine a piece of cloth making such a difference in a person's whole appearance!

Ricky was strolling about the room, examining everything intently. "Is your father going to wear a formal jacket?" she asked in surprise, looking at a white jacket with a stylish shawl collar.

"Oh yes," answered Donna, matter-of-factly. "In India everyone dresses for dinner, especially at the *better hotels.*" She accented the last two words and cast a sidelong glance at the other girl. Yes, Ricky was really impressed.

"What else does your mother have to do, Don?" Ricky asked. "I don't see how she could take more clothes than she has here, especially in an airplane."

"It's not so much, really, and she had a lot of the things already. Now she has to get me ready."

"You?" Ricky looked at her in surprise. "Are you getting new clothes, too?"

"Of course not, silly. But don't forget, there's a lot to running a house. Mommy said she'd cook some things for us and put them in Mrs. Gray's freezer. You know, stews and spaghetti sauce and chicken casseroles. Then all we'll have to do is heat them."

"That's a good idea," agreed Ricky.

"And we're going to plan all the menus so Miss Dengrove and I will know what to buy each week."

"If you need someone to drive you to the supermarket, I'm sure my mother will be glad to take you," offered Ricky.

"Thanks, Rick. But Miss Dengrove can drive, and Daddy said he'd let her use our car. He said it would be much better than having it sit in the garage and letting the battery run down."

"That's wonderful, Donna. Maybe she'll even drive us part of the way to school in the morning."

Donna shook her head. "Not unless you want to leave half an hour earlier than we do now. Miss Dengrove says that she's usually the first one in school in the morning. She's awfully anxious to do a good job, and she's always doing extra things like making charts and putting drawings on the blackboard. I think one of the reasons my mother and father like her so much is that she tries so hard to do everything just right."

"But she's fun to be with, too, isn't she?"

"Oh, yes." Donna smoothed the fringe on the mane of her nondescript animal. The red flannel was getting worn in spots, but it was still her favorite stuffed toy. Miss Dengrove had told her about a pattern for a darling giraffe she could make out of gingham, and had promised to help her with it.

"Isn't it wonderful how things have worked out, Ricky? I can't even see any problems ahead."

Mrs. Parker, however, could see quite a few.

"Something's been troubling me for several days, Donna," her mother said later that afternoon. "What are we going to do about your money?"

"You mean my allowance, Mommy? Oh, I guess you could give it all to me before you leave, and I'll take out a little each week. Won't that be all right?"

"And what about the household money, dear?" Mrs. Parker asked. "You'll have to buy groceries and pay the milkman and all sorts of things. I was thinking—" she paused, hand on hip.

"Yes, Mommy?" Donna was thoughtful. Goodness, she

hadn't considered the fact that she or Miss Dengrove would have to pay bills. Well, maybe her mother was beginning to think she was more grown-up at last.

"Donna, suppose I make out a series of checks, one for each week I'm gone. You can cash them at the bank because they know you there. In that way, you won't have too much cash lying around the house at one time. Just be sure you put the money in a safe place, and don't lose it."

Oh, jeepers, thought Donna, there she went again, acting as though I didn't have any idea of the value of money. Why did she have to say things like that?

"As for the checks, I'll put them in a special envelope and mark it some way. And I'll tack it on a corner of the bulletin board here in the kitchen so it won't get mislaid in a drawer someplace. I know, I'll mark the envelope with some of that red cellophane tape that was left over from Christmas. That'll be bright enough to catch your eye so you won't ever make a mistake about the envelope. I'll also put an envelope on the bulletin board with checks for the cleaning woman who will be here once a week. Are you listening, Donna?"

"Yes, Mother," was the polite reply. But inwardly, Donna was seething. Marking envelopes with red tape.

Imagine! The way you would mark something for a baby. Why wasn't she old enough to have a checking account of her own so they wouldn't have to go through all this nonsense?

"Remember to tell Miss Dengrove about this, Donna. She refuses to let me pay her for staying with you, because she says she'll be so glad to be living in a real home again. But I'd feel just dreadful if she spent any of her own money."

"Yes, Mother," said Donna dutifully, only half listening again. Oh, things would be different when Miss Dengrove came. Of course she loved her mother and all that, but wouldn't it be wonderful not to have to listen to orders and instructions and nagging all the time. The next two weeks couldn't go too quickly to suit her!

Almost before she knew it, the day before departure was there. The suitcases were packed, the passports and visas ready, the meals planned, the food cooked and in Mrs. Gray's freezer, and a thousand instructions given.

"I'd feel much better if Miss Dengrove could come tonight," said Mrs. Parker to Donna after dinner, as she put some extra tissues in the handbag she was going to carry. "But I could hardly ask her to sleep on the living room sofa. I knew it was foolish to take that couch out of the little sewing room when Uncle Roger left, because now there's no place for an overnight guest to stay."

"That's all right, Mommy. She said she'd be over first thing in the morning. And your plane doesn't leave until late in the afternoon. It's lucky you're going on a Saturday, so we don't have to go to school."

"Your father and I will have to take a very early train to New York, you know, Donna, and then get the airline bus out to Idlewild Airport." Mrs. Parker sighed and surveyed her bedroom. "I can't think of a single thing I haven't done. Remember, dear, I put the telephone numbers of all the repairmen in the book with the menus."

"I wish you wouldn't worry so, Mommy," said Donna. "We'll manage perfectly well."

"Yes, dear, I'm sure that you will. But you know that I have to worry about something."

"Then worry about the weather." Donna moved the bedroom curtains aside and peered at a dark sky. "I can't see a single star tonight, Mommy. And it's gotten awfully cold, hasn't it? Isn't it usually warmer than this at the end of March?"

"It was certainly warmer two weeks ago when you wanted to go on an overnight hike," laughed Mrs. Parker. "How would you like to be sleeping outdoors tonight?"

Donna shivered. "No, thank you. Oh, well, the sun will probably be shining brightly by morning."

When morning came, however, and Donna poked her nose out from under the covers, there was not a single ray of sunshine in her usually cheerful room. She ran to the window, then let out a little shriek. She raced into the front bedroom, and finding that empty, ran barefoot downstairs.

"Oh, Mommy, isn't this dreadful! Did you look outside?"

Mr. and Mrs. Parker were drinking their morning coffee, and appeared very solemn.

"It's been snowing all night," Mr. Parker said. "And it seems that it's not going to stop. We've been calling the weather bureau every few minutes since we got up."

"Are the planes leaving, Daddy?" Donna asked.

"The airline says there's a slight delay, but they are taking off. The trains to New York are pretty close to schedule, too. Our problem is to get to the station. There's not a car out, and even the cabs aren't running."

"How will Miss Dengrove get here?" asked Donna,

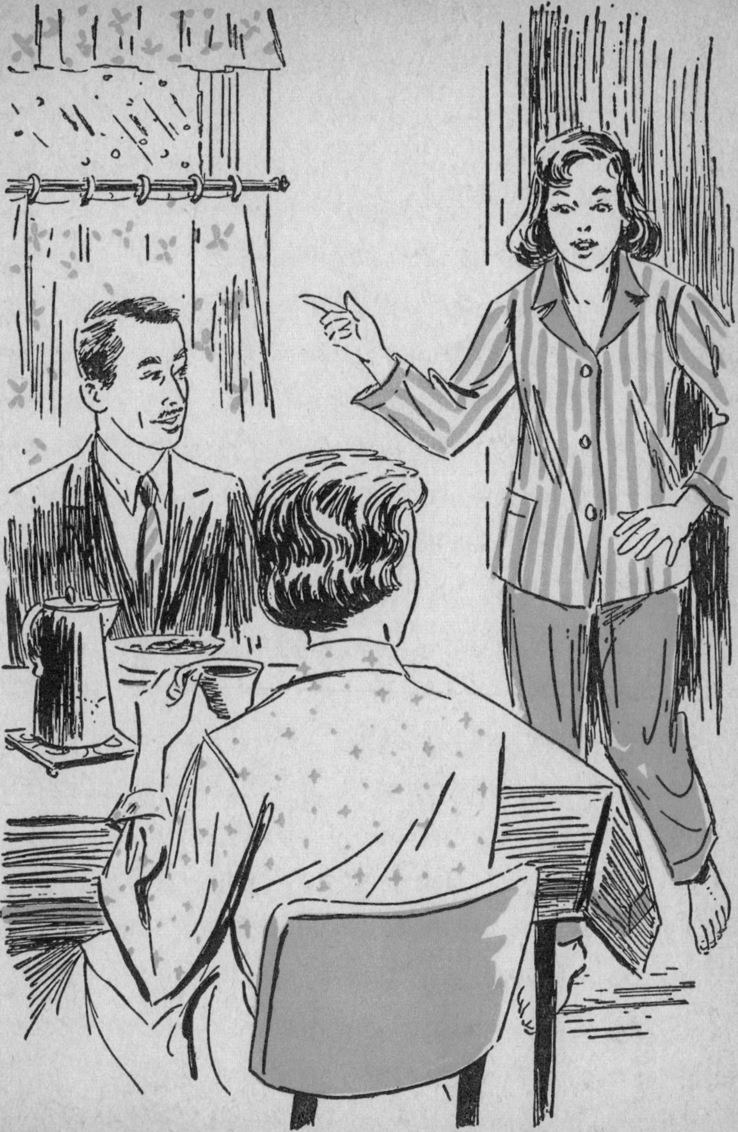

upset by this unforeseen turn of events.

"Her call woke us this morning," explained Mrs. Parker. "She's been trying to get a cab for ever so long. They say that four taxis are stranded in the snow, and they can't take a chance on sending any more out."

"What'll we do?" wailed Donna, going to the living-room window. "You're right—there isn't a single car out there," she called. "Oh, Mommy, you can't miss the plane just because of a crazy old snowstorm." She returned to the kitchen.

Mrs. Parker smiled wanly. "We'll keep trying, Donna. We'll be ready to leave in a little while. I don't see how we can go, though, until Miss Dengrove gets here."

Mr. and Mrs. Parker went upstairs to finish their last-minute packing. Donna went back to the living-room window. There was utter stillness outside, and the world looked fresh and new and crystal cold.

"Like one of those glass paperweights that you shake and there's a whole snow storm inside," she thought, shivering a little. Instead of going upstairs to get her bathrobe and slippers, she put on an old coat from the hall closet, then went back to watching the soft flurries of white.

Mrs. Parker came downstairs. Her husband followed

with two suitcases. "I'll try that cab company once more," he said. "I'm afraid our own car would get stuck in a snowdrift and we'd be worse off than before."

"Mommy, Daddy, look!" Donna cried. "Here comes the little truck from Chip's Meat Market. It's got chains on, but at least it's moving. Maybe the driver would take you to the station."

Mr. Parker dashed coatless down the steps, and Donna and her mother could see him signaling frantically to the driver. Then there was a moment's conversation, and Mr. Parker reappeared in the living room, shedding snow in little rivulets.

"Donna, my dear, you deserve a medal! That was a brilliant suggestion." Donna beamed. Her father turned to Mrs. Parker.

"That nice boy, Sandy Something-or-other, is driving. He says he's pretty sure he can get us to the station. That old truck is as good as a bulldozer. Sure you don't mind sitting on the front seat, honey?"

Mrs. Parker shook her head. "I'd stand on the running board if necessary, Sam. We're really in luck. But how about—"

"I was coming to that. He says that after he takes us,

he'll pick up Miss Dengrove and bring her here. Says he's sure the boss won't mind. There's no one in the store now, anyhow. Isn't that nice of him?"

"Oh, wonderful, wonderful. Donna, you call Miss Dengrove and tell her. We'll telephone from New York and make sure everything's all right here before we leave. Sam, do you have everything?" Mrs. Parker buttoned her overshoes, and picked up her handbag.

"Jimmy, Jimmy!" Mr. Parker called from the bottom of the stairs. "We're leaving! Hurry!"

A tousled head appeared over the banister.

"Okay, Pop! I'm up."

"Good-by, Jimmy," said Mrs. Parker, going up a few steps to kiss her son and give him a last tight squeeze. "Be a good boy!" Then she turned to her daughter. "Donna, get his breakfast for him, please. And try to have the beds made before Miss Dengrove gets here. Oh, dear, oh, dear, I'm sure I'm forgetting something."

"Now relax, honey," said Mr. Parker. "We've got everything. Good-by, Donna dear," he said, kissing the top of his daughter's head. "We'll miss you."

"Good-by, Cooky," said Mrs. Parker, hugging her daughter. Donna thought she detected a watery brightness in her mother's eyes. "Now don't forget to write. You have all our hotel addresses in that black book. And don't forget about taking care of the money."

"I'll do everything, Mommy. Have fun. And don't worry, please. Everything will be fine."

"Come on, come on," called Mr. Parker impatiently from the front door. "That Sandy boy can't wait all day."

Mrs. Parker drew her coat tighter around her and followed her husband out the door and into the delivery truck.

Donna watched, nose pressed against the glass, until the truck turned a corner and was gone.

Then she sighed and trudged slowly up the stairs to dress. She probably had an hour or so until Miss Dengrove arrived. Goodness, everything was quiet. Jimmy must have gone back to bed.

The stillness in the house seemed to echo the stillness of the world outdoors. She could almost hear the snowflakes landing on the roof. Utter, complete, absolute silence.

She walked soundlessly to her closet and dug her head into a corner to find her dungarees. And there, with half her body in the closet and half out, her heart jumped. Something was going to happen.

"*Crooak,*" came a loud, raucous sound.

What could it have been? Maybe she was imagining it. Sometimes silence played tricks on your ears.

No—there it was again!

"*Crooak.*" Was it a door groaning, or an animal? It seemed to come from below her, but was it in the house or outside? Certainly it was a sound she had never heard before. But maybe it had stopped, or gone away.

"Hey, Sis!" Jimmy's face peered in at her bedroom door. "What's that horrible noise? It sounds like nothin' human!"

CHAPTER 5   *This Is Living!*

Donna stood quite still, clutching her dungarees. She must stay calm. If only her father were here and she could call, "Daddy, what's that crazy sound?" And he would answer, "Just a minute, honey, I'll look and see." But there was no one to call. She, Donna Parker, was in charge.

She bit her lower lip. "Oh, I'm sure it's nothing, Jimmy. Maybe there's a cat outside. Cats make all sorts of weird noises, you know. Why, sometimes in the middle of the night they sound just like babies crying."

Jimmy looked at his sister incredulously. "A cat? Who're you kiddin'? Dontcha think I know a cat when I hear one? Anyhow, I'll bet you anything that noise came from inside this house."

"Well, it's gone now." Donna could almost smile. "We haven't heard it again, have we?"

Jimmy shook his head, then shrugged his shoulders. "I guess I'd better get dressed. Soon as it stops snowing, I'll get Skipper and we'll have a snowball fight."

He pattered down the hall to his room. Donna sank down on her bed. And at that moment the sound came again.

"*Crooak, crooak.*"

Almost at the same instant, Jimmy was back in her room. "See, see," he whispered. "There it goes again. It is in this house! Come on, Sis, let's go see what it is."

Donna nodded. "All right, Jimmy. I—I guess we ought to. Wait till I get on my robe and slippers."

Together they tiptoed down the steps, scarcely daring to breathe. All was still. There was a faint hiss of steam from the pipes, and in the quiet they could hear the refrigerator motor turn on.

The front door was still closed tight, and there was no sign of life in the living room. Donna looked out the window and could see only faint traces of the footprints made by her mother and father in the snow. The new flakes were quickly obliterating all marks.

"Nothing in the dining room either, Sis," whispered Jimmy. "Come on, let's try the kitchen."

But there, too, everything seemed in order. Donna breathed a sigh of relief.

"Well, whatever it was must have gone away by now. Get dressed, Jimmy, and I'll make your breakfast. Miss Dengrove will be here pretty soon."

"Maybe it was just the wind makin' a shutter creak, or somethin'," agreed Jimmy.

And then, without warning, very much louder and closer than before, came the sound again!

"Crooak, crooak."

They both jumped, startled. "It's—it's on the b-b-back porch," stammered Jimmy.

To his amazement, Donna laughed. "Of course, silly, that's what it is."

"What's what it is?" asked Jimmy, realizing he was not making sense.

But Donna did not answer. Instead, she opened the door to the back porch and beckoned to her brother.

"Ooh, it's freezing out here," he said, his teeth chattering partly from cold and partly from fright.

"Look!" Donna pointed to one end of the small room. There was her white dove, huddled in a corner of its cage, feathers ruffled, head drawn back into its body as far as it would go. And as they watched, the throat of the dove swelled, and it called, *"Crooak."*

"Hey, that's pretty dumb," said Jimmy. "Why didn't we think of the dove?" He scratched his head. "But isn't that a queer noise for a dove to make? I thought they just cooed sometimes, sort of like pigeons."

"I thought so, too," said Donna. "In fact, this one hardly ever does even that. It's been such a quiet bird that it never occurred to me that it could make such a loud noise."

They ran back into the kitchen, and Donna closed the door carefully behind her. "Ooh, it's cold out there," she said, rubbing her hands together.

"You know what I think, Jimmy?" she asked as they walked up the stairs to their rooms again. "I think that it got awfully cold on the porch last night, and my dove caught cold. I guess that noise must be the way doves cough. I wonder if it ought to have some medicine or something."

But what with getting breakfast for herself and her brother, cleaning the kitchen, and making her bed and seeing that Jimmy made his, Donna had little time to worry about the bird.

Occasionally the loud raucous noise would send her out

to the back porch. When she had finished straightening up, she put an old piece of flannel around the cage to keep out the drafts, which seemed to make the bird a little more comfortable. "At least I don't think it's coughing so much," Donna murmured. Then she could think of nothing else to do.

"I do wish Miss Dengrove would get here," she thought when she had inspected the house once more and felt it would meet the teacher's approval. Again she took up her station at the front window in the living room. For several minutes she entertained herself by drawing pictures with her finger in the misty spots her breath left on the glass.

"Here she comes, Jimmy!" she called a little later, erasing her initials and a game of ticktacktoe from the window. She watched as the little truck with CHIP'S MEAT MARKET lettered on the side stopped in front of the Parker house.

Miss Dengrove ran up the front steps carrying a suitcase. She was still stamping snow off her boots when Donna opened the door.

The young woman stepped in and shook her hair to remove the light dusting of snowflakes.

"Well," she sighed, and smiled brightly at Donna. "Did you think I'd never get here? I was so sorry not to be here when your parents left. Isn't this a dreadful state of affairs?"

"I'm glad you came when you did," said Donna, hanging up the teacher's coat and trying to act like a gracious hostess. "Did the truck have trouble getting through?"

Miss Dengrove shook her head. "No, we managed very nicely. But there are ever so many cars stranded in the streets. Some of them are covered with so much snow that they look like little white hills."

"I'll show you your room," offered Donna, picking up the teacher's suitcase and leading the way up the stairs. "Mommy changed the sheets this morning before she left. She put all her dresses in the sewing room so you could use her closet, and she said that the two top drawers in her bureau are for you. Do you think that'll be enough room?"

"When I brought only that little suitcase? More than enough, Donna. I really intended to bring all my things, but because of the weather my landlady said I could leave the rest of my clothes there for a few days. But even then, I'm sure I'll be very comfortable here."

The young woman looked around her. "Oh, it'll be so wonderful not to feel cooped up. I can't wait to get into a real kitchen again, instead of eating those dreadful restaurant meals."

"Do you like to cook?" asked Donna.

"You couldn't really call it cooking," laughed Miss Dengrove. "But I love to make things for parties, and—" she hesitated. "Tell you what, Donna. It's such a dismal day, we should do something to cheer us up. Suppose I put my things away, and get into a pair of slacks, and then we'll make some fudge! Does your mother have cooking chocolate?"

Donna nodded, her eyes sparkling. "I'm sure she does. I'll run down and see."

Wasn't this wonderful? Instead of having to clean out closets, or sew missing buttons on her blouses, she and Miss Dengrove would make fudge! Wait'll she told Ricky!

Yes, there was the baking chocolate in the cupboard. What else would they need? Sugar, vanilla, milk, butter, a saucepan, a spoon for stirring. Donna opened and closed cupboard doors, humming a little tune.

In a few minutes, Miss Dengrove joined her in the kitchen. "I peeped into Jimmy's room and asked him if he'd like to help, too," said the teacher. "He's washing his hands."

Oh, dear, thought Donna. Why did he have to interfere? Jimmy never wanted to do anything in the kitchen. Now, just because he liked Miss Dengrove, he'd probably be hanging around like a puppy dog all the time, and they would never have a chance to be alone.

But even with Jimmy there, making fudge was fun.

"Some day I'll treat myself to a candy thermometer," said Miss Dengrove, dropping a bit of the chocolate into a cup of cold water. "Donna, does that look like the soft-ball stage to you?"

Donna inspected the cup thoughtfully. "I think it's just about right now," she nodded.

She watched as Miss Dengrove beat the wonderful smelling mixture and poured it into the pan which she had carefully greased. Then Donna put the filled pan on the little table on the back porch.

"It'll cool quickly out there," she said. "Jimmy, do you want to lick the spoon or the bowl?"

"Bowl, bowl," cried her brother.

As Donna took one spoon and offered the other one to Miss Dengrove, the phone rang.

"I'll get it," she said. "Oh, I hope it's Mommy and Daddy."

"One moment, please," said the operator's voice. "Go ahead, please."

"It is," whispered Donna, protecting the phone from

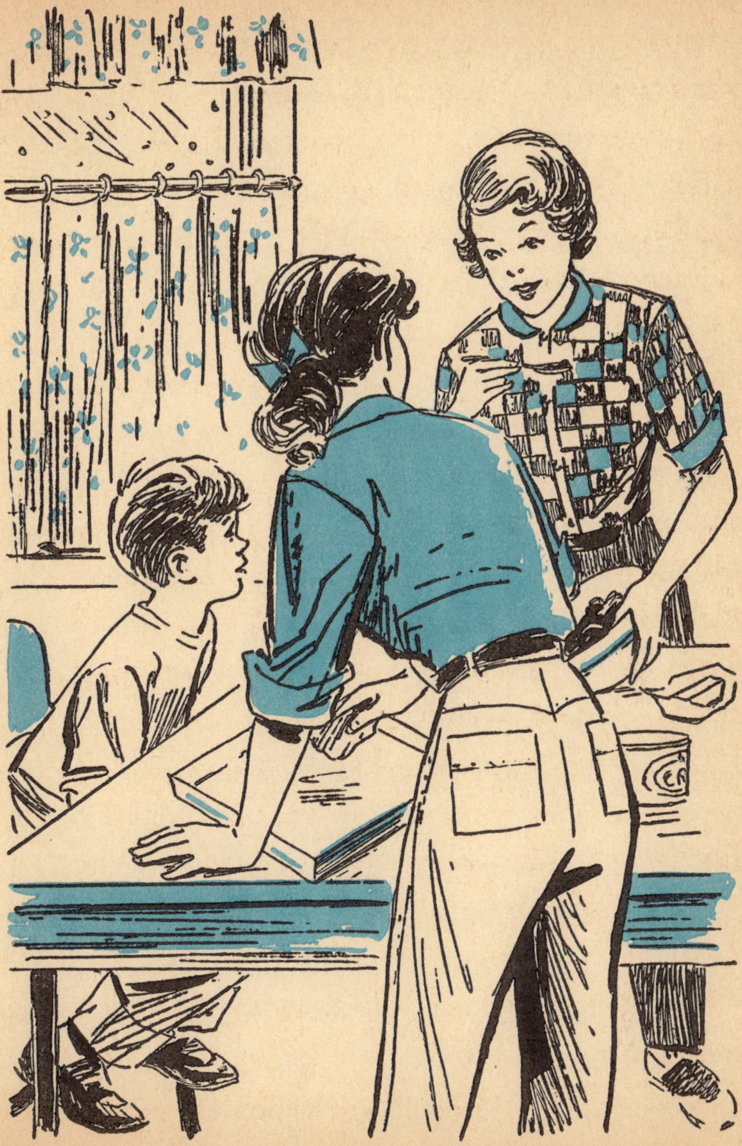

Jimmy's expected rush. But Jimmy was much too busy scraping chocolate with his finger to pay attention to a telephone call.

"Hello, Mommy?" said Donna when she heard the familiar voice. "Did you get to New York all right? Where are you now? At the airport? Are the planes leaving all right? Well, a slight delay isn't too bad. Yes, it's still snowing here."

She paused for a moment. "Yes, we're fine. Miss Dengrove came a little while after you left. Yes, I made the beds, and I cleaned the kitchen, too." Goodness, even at this distance her mother was checking up on her. "Oh, we just made fudge with Miss Dengrove. We'll have lunch in a little while. We had a late breakfast, you know, Mommy." Yeeks, she was leaving her for six weeks, but she didn't even trust her to know when it was time to eat lunch!

"Please don't worry, Mommy. I told you we'll manage very nicely. Jimmy's being very good. All right, I'll tell her. Have a good time."

Donna hung up slowly. The full import of what was happening struck her suddenly. Her mother and father would get on an airplane in a few minutes, and she probably wouldn't hear from them again until they were on the other side of the world.

"Oh, Miss Dengrove, Mother reminded me to tell you about the house money." She explained about the system of weekly checks, and showed the teacher the envelope, marked with a wide border of bright red cellophane tape, that was tacked to the upper corner of the bulletin board. "She left a few dollars in the cooky jar over there, too, in case we needed something before we could get to the bank. That's where she always keeps money for paying the paper boy and things like that." She paused to see if she had remembered all the messages.

"And Mommy said please not to spend your own money for anything," added Donna. "She was so glad that you were able to stay with us. It certainly wouldn't be right for you to have to pay for food and things. And we're glad that you came, too." She gave the young woman a quick hug.

"I wish you'd do something for me, Donna," said the teacher. "Please don't call me Miss Dengrove. I get enough of that at school. I'd very much like you to call me Marjorie."

"I'll try," said Donna shyly, realizing that the teacher

had suggested this once before. She looked at Miss Dengrove. Dressed in a bright checkered shirt and gray flannel slacks, and wearing a pair of saddle shoes, she certainly didn't look much older than Donna.

"It'll be a little strange at first, but the name does seem to fit you—Marjorie."

"And now, lunch," said the teacher briskly. "I hope you haven't stuffed yourselves with so much fudge that you've lost your appetites."

Lunch, too, was fun. Everyone merely helped himself to whatever caught his fancy in the refrigerator.

"This is much nicer than the same old soup and sandwich and milk that we get every Saturday," said Donna contentedly, mixing some cold spaghetti with a little tuna fish on her plate.

"It's what the Swedish restaurants call a *smorgasbord*," explained the teacher. "They have dozens of platters on a table, buffet style, and you help yourself to a little of whatever you want. Only I don't see any sense in taking all the dishes out of the refrigerator and then putting them back." She took a bite of her peanut butter, jelly, and green pepper sandwich.

"What'll we do this afternoon, huh?" asked Jimmy,

taking a swipe at his mouth with the back of his sleeve.

"Jimmy!" scolded Donna. "You know you have to use a napkin to wipe your mouth."

"I thought that by now the sun would be out," said Miss Dengrove, "but it seems to be snowing harder than ever. So I guess we'll have to stay in the house and read, or find something else to do. Let's just leave the dishes in the sink and do them with the supper dishes."

The thought had never occurred to Donna. Mother certainly has me well-trained, she said to herself, as she scraped the few dishes they had used and left them in the sink. What a wonderful way to live! It was certainly more relaxing than the constant cleaning and cooking and washing that her mother did.

"Do you mind if I use the phone for a while?" Donna asked the teacher. "I'd like to call a few of my friends." This was the opportunity she had been waiting for. No one to say, "Donna, you've talked long enough," or, "Donna, someone may be trying to call us."

"Go right ahead," said Miss Dengrove. "I might take a little nap."

Ricky seemed glad to hear from her, and was delighted that things were working out so well. Donna gave her all the details of the Parkers' departure in the morning, the arrival of the teacher, the making of the fudge, and the wonderfully informal lunch. But at that point Ricky said her mother was calling her—she would have to hang up.

Then Donna called, in turn, Anne and Karen and Mary, and told them the events of the day. They discussed the snowstorm and school affairs, until each of the girls apologized and said she had things to do. Finally Donna even called Joyce Davenport, who was still the editor of the junior high school paper, the *Summerfield Sum-It-Up*.

"She's been ever so much nicer since she broke her leg this winter," recalled Donna as she dialed Joyce's number. "It's hard to realize that we all used to think she was stuck-up—just because she was smart, and acted bossy because she didn't know how to make friends."

Joyce, too, was glad to hear from Donna. "Maybe you can come over to my house one day after school," Joyce said, still with a trace of uncertainty in her voice, as though she couldn't believe that she was really accepted by the girls.

"I'd love to," Donna answered, and then the conversation dragged, until Donna herself at last said she had to hang up.

For a while she looked through the magazines in the living room. Then she went up to her bedroom, turned on her little radio, and lay on the floor while she listened to dance tunes. This was living!

Miss Dengrove was still in her room, napping or perhaps reading. Jimmy, apparently, was having a good time with his toy soldiers, for Donna could hear him giving orders, booming imaginary artillery, and zooming his airplanes over the hapless lead figures.

"Isn't it funny?" thought Donna after a while. "This is what I've been looking forward to for so long—being alone like this, and able to do whatever I want. And now I can't think of a single thing to do! Well, maybe the sun will be shining tomorrow, and we'll be able to go out and have fun in the snow."

To everyone's dismay, however, Sunday was as dreary a day as Saturday had been.

"This is absolutely amazing!" said Miss Dengrove at breakfast. "I have never heard of a snowstorm so late in the year. And such a snowstorm!"

Jimmy stuffed a forkful of pancakes into his mouth. "You can't even see the front steps," he mumbled, but his eyes were shining. "Isn't that sumpin'? The snow comes all the way up to the front porch. I bet we'll have to wear snowshoes when we go out, 'cause otherwise we'll practically drown, like in quicksand."

"I do hope Mother and Daddy got across the ocean all right," worried Donna.

Miss Dengrove patted her hand. "Now don't you fret, honey. Airplanes fly above the weather, and a little old snow storm doesn't mean a thing to them."

"Boy, it looks like it's *never* gonna stop!" said Jimmy. "Well, guess I'll go play with my soldiers some more. We had a real good battle yesterday—only three men left out of the whole battalion."

"I heard you." Donna grimaced. "If you must play those silly games, Jimmy, please be a little quieter. Marjorie and I will get headaches from all your banging and clanging."

"Oh, it doesn't bother me," smiled Miss Dengrove. "I know boys have to make a certain amount of noise."

Jimmy swaggered off, and Donna volunteered to do the breakfast dishes. "At least it'll give me something to do," the girl thought.

For a while, the rattling of dishes was the only sound in the house. Then Donna became conscious of another kind of noise.

"Oh, my bird!" she thought. "My poor bird. There it goes again. Did it stop the croaking yesterday, or did I just get used to it? No, I'm sure it's louder now."

When the dishes were finished, she refilled the water and seed dishes in the cage.

"I'm going to bring you in the kitchen," she whispered to the bird. "Mommy wouldn't like it, I know, but I can't have you freezing out here. Oh, I should have brought you in last night. Wasn't that thoughtless of me?"

The warm room, however, seemed to have no effect on the bird's condition. The cough, or whatever the noise was, was definitely worse.

"Between the dove and Jimmy, I think I'll go out of my mind," thought Donna by afternoon. "If it isn't the croaking from the kitchen, it's the clatter from upstairs. Goodness, I can't even read."

At that moment the telephone rang loudly.

"I'll get it," Donna called. "It's probably one of the girls."

But when she picked up the receiver the voice at the other end of the line said, "This is Western Union. We have not been able to deliver your wire by messenger boy because of weather conditions, but if you'd like, we will send you a confirming wire."

"But what's it about?" asked Donna breathlessly.

"This is a cable signed 'Mother and Daddy.' It was sent from Paris, France."

"From Paris?" Donna repeated aloud. "But they were supposed to go right on to Rome. Oh, goodness, I wonder what the trouble is now."

CHAPTER 6   *Problems*

Miss Dengrove, who had hurried downstairs, handed Donna a pencil and a piece of paper. "Write it down," she whispered.

Donna nodded gratefully. "Will you repeat that, please?" she asked the operator. "I'd like to write the message."

There was a moment's silence as Donna's pencil moved. Then she put the receiver in place and read the words aloud. " 'Arrived Paris safely. Rome tonight. Love Mother and Daddy.' "

She looked up at Miss Dengrove and heaved a sigh of relief. "I guess everything's all right. They told me they'd be in Rome by Sunday night, and I guess Paris was just a stopover. Goodness, I was worried for a minute."

"Now all we have to worry about is the snowstorm," said Miss Dengrove. Donna walked into the living room with her, and together they looked out the window. The sky was still a pale gray, and large white flakes were dropping slowly to the ground.

"I think it's letting up a little," the teacher said. "But even if it stops completely, I'll bet we don't have school tomorrow."

Sure enough, Donna awoke on Monday morning to the sound of whistles blowing. "No school," she thought, and buried her head deeper under the blankets. "At least I can sleep late."

But sleep would not come, and finally Donna dressed and went downstairs. She busied herself making breakfast for everyone, and at last the smells of coffee and bacon awoke Miss Dengrove and Jimmy.

"Oh, this is wonderful of you, Donna," Marjorie yawned as she came into the kitchen. "I would have slept all day if I hadn't smelled this yummy food."

"I wish I *had* slept all day," grumbled Jimmy. "Nothin' to do today again."

"Oh, oh," thought his sister. "If Jimmy can't find things to occupy himself, he's going to be a real nuisance. Here comes trouble." But if Donna had only known, she would have worried more about her own boredom than Jimmy's.

Not until many weeks later was she to learn that the ever-widening circles of her problems had begun on this day, and she alone was to blame for them. Now, though, the only thing that concerned her was her brother.

Whatever she suggested to entertain him, from cutting out pictures of automobiles to toasting marshmallows in the fireplace, did not meet with his approval.

"I just want to play ball," he insisted. And despite the objections of Donna and Marjorie, he went down to the basement and began hitting his baseball against the wall.

"*Thump, thump, thump, thump,*" went the constant refrain, until Donna could feel it like a hammer pounding in her brain.

"Now you just stop that, James Parker," she called down the basement stairs. "Or I'll come down and make you stop."

"Oh, yeah?" was the answer, followed by another *thump*.

"Just a minute, Donna," said Marjorie. "Let me try talking to him again. Apparently baseball is awfully important to him."

"Jimmy," she called. "Will you come here for a minute? I'd like to talk to you about Mr. Curtin."

"Who?"

"Mr. Curtin. You know, your baseball coach."

"What about?" But there was a dragging of footsteps on the stairs, and, ball in hand, Jimmy appeared upstairs.

"You like baseball a great deal, don't you?" asked Miss Dengrove.

"Sure." Jimmy's tone announced that he was suspicious of the entire conversation.

"And Mr. Curtin comes over from the junior high school several days a week to help the boys in our school, doesn't he? And pretty soon he'll be picking the team?"

Jimmy nodded to each question, and tossed the ball from hand to hand.

"Well, I know Mr. Curtin pretty well. We sometimes have lunch together."

"Yeah?" Jimmy looked up with a so-what expression on his face.

"I'm sure he's told you how important co-operation is to a team. Now you wouldn't want me to tell Mr. Curtin that you're not co-operative, would you?"

"Why would you do that?" Jimmy's eyes widened.

"I realize that it's hard for you to stay in the house so long," the teacher explained. "But see if you can't find something to do that's a little quieter than army games or

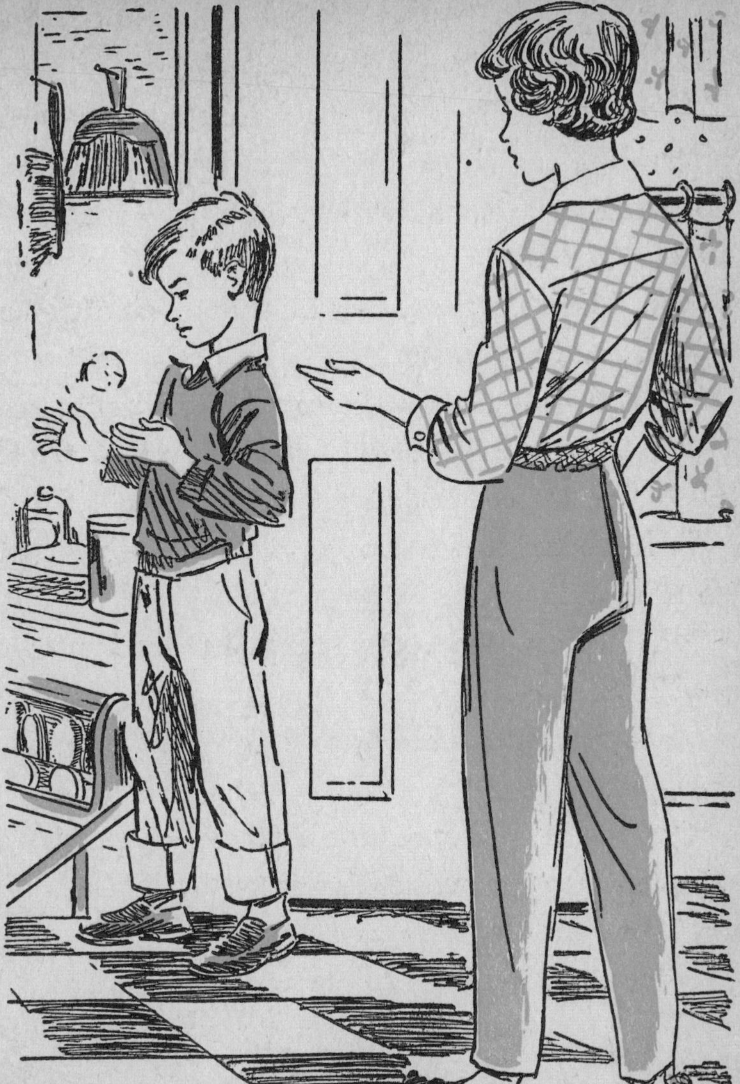

ball-playing, won't you? A little more team spirit, you know?"

"I just wanna play ball a little," Jimmy muttered, but he went upstairs to his room.

"Thanks, Marjorie," said Donna. "Now maybe we'll have a little peace and quiet."

As though on signal, the dove began to croak. "Oh, I think I'll go out of my mind," Donna cried, as she jumped from her chair. "Maybe I ought to call Ricky and talk to her," she thought as Marjorie went up to her room to escape.

"I don't know what to do," Donna wailed to her friend. "I thought it would be such fun with Miss Dengrove here, and instead I'm bored to tears. Jimmy's a nuisance, and my dove keeps making dreadful noises. Oh, I wish you could come over."

"It's this awful snow," Ricky replied. "You'll start having fun when you can get out. My mother has me cleaning silver, of all things. You know how I hate that! Just when I was reading a simply marvelous book about Africa."

"About Africa?" Ricky did read the queerest things.

"Oh, it's wonderful, Don. About this woman who goes on a safari in the jungle, to get elephants and tigers and things for a circus, because she's an animal trainer, and she has a monkey that does all sorts of wonderful tricks."

"A woman animal trainer?"

"Oh, sure, women are the best ones because they have so much patience and understanding. I wish I had an animal I could teach—"

"But, Ricky," Donna interrupted. "You don't even like animals."

Ricky stopped short. "But—this is different, Donna." She paused. "No, I guess you're right. I always get these crazy notions." Then in a more animated tone, "But you'd be wonderful, Don. Wouldn't you love being an animal trainer, standing in the center of a cage, dressed in red satin tights and surrounded by lions, and thousands of people sitting breathless while you crack your whip?"

Donna giggled. "Can't you picture me training lions, Ricky? My mother won't even let me have a dog in this house. Only a dove that keeps croaking and cawing."

"Well, you just have to begin with what you've got," argued Ricky. "Why don't you start by teaching your dove to do things? Birds shouldn't be too hard to train, and you're good with animals."

"It's easy for you to talk," Donna thought when Ricky

had hung up. "I wouldn't have the faintest idea how to begin."

She went over to the cage, which was still where she had left it on the kitchen floor. Then she shrugged her shoulders, opened the little wire door, and gently drew out the bird. "I don't have anything else to do," she thought. "I may as well try it."

The bird shuddered in her hand, and she smoothed the ruffled feathers.

She placed the dove on the kitchen table. Immediately it flapped its wings and flew about the room. "Now come here," she commanded, but the bird paid no heed and continued its flight.

"Poor birdie," Donna said aloud. "You don't like being cooped up in a cage any more than I like being cooped up in this house. My mother and father are the only ones who are doing any flying. You and I have to stay in one place."

If she only could have gone to India, she thought, forgetting that she had decided that it would be more fun to stay with Miss Dengrove, forgetting all the arguments against her going, and remembering only that she had been left behind.

"Well, I won't be snowbound all the time," she resolved. "And when I get out, then I'll have a good time, no matter what I have to do. Come on, birdie, let's get on with the tricks."

The dove perched on the top of a cupboard and stared unblinkingly at her.

"I ought to hold something in my hand for it to eat," Donna thought. But neither crackers nor lettuce nor cornflakes tempted the bird.

She sat down at the kitchen table and picked up a magazine. "I will not go climbing after that stupid bird," she thought. "As soon as I get near it, it'll fly someplace else. So it can just sit up there, for all I care."

But out of the corner of her eye, she watched it as it flew to another cupboard, then to a counter top, then picked its way among the flour and sugar canisters to the sink. It stopped a moment, then flew over to the other side of the room past the bulletin board, brushing its wings against the various papers that were pasted there.

Just as Donna was about to give up in disgust, it lighted on the kitchen table. She put the magazine down quietly and watched the bird. It seemed fascinated by the magazine.

"I know! It likes the bright colors in the pictures,"

Donna thought. With a little hop, the bird landed on the magazine and diligently proceeded to claw the page to pieces.

"I'll try another one to make sure," Donna thought, and went to get another magazine. When she returned, the bird seemed to be sitting in a bed of confetti. "Now, look what it did to that!" She laughed aloud. "Maybe we could hire it out to make confetti for parties."

She put the other magazine on the table and began to turn the pages loudly. The bird, attracted by the noise, turned and seemed to be looking at her. When she moved away, the dove hopped over to the new magazine and began the scratching process again. Donna watched, delighted.

Suddenly she felt someone's presence in the room. Looking up, she saw Jimmy in the doorway.

"Wow-ie!" he exclaimed. "Looka this place. It's a good thing Mom isn't here. That dopey old bird isn't supposed to be in the kitchen anyhow. And what's all this stuff?" He picked up a handful of various things from the counter. "Lettuce, and crackers, and cornflakes all over the place. And that mess all over the table. You'd better clean it up, fast."

Donna turned on her brother hotly. "You don't have

to tell me what to do, Jimmy Parker. I'm a lot older than you and I know when a room has to be cleaned and when it doesn't. So please go away now."

Jimmy helped himself to some cookies and strolled off. Donna continued to watch the bird shredding paper.

"I think that's enough training for now," she thought after a while. Carefully she picked up the dove, put it back in the cage, and closed the door. As the wire snapped, the bird began its croaking again.

"Poor birdie," Donna said again. "We don't like to be shut up, do we? We ought to be out trying our wings and seeing the world." She felt she was talking to herself as much as to the bird.

She looked around her. The room really looked dreadful. "Well," she thought resentfully, "at least there's no one here to keep telling me to clean up. And I like it this way! I'm tired of living in a house where everything has to be just so. I like a *lived-in* look!"

She strode out of the kitchen, leaving everything the way it was.

"And that kitchen certainly does look lived-in," she thought wryly. "Mother would have a fit! I'm glad Marjorie doesn't care."

CHAPTER 7 *Five Dollars*

Donna sat bolt upright in her bed. "Well," she said aloud. "I never thought I'd live to see the sun shining again."

But here it was, pouring into her room on a beautiful Tuesday morning. The weather forecasters on the radio the night before had promised that the snow would end during the night. It had been the heaviest snowfall in that part of the state in fifty years, they had said. Of course there would be no school, because the roads were not yet passable.

But the sky this morning was the clear blue of a baby's eyes, and the snow looked like soft woolly nursery blankets. "I'll certainly get outside today," thought Donna jubilantly. "Oh, I can't wait to feel some fresh air on my face."

Then she stopped and listened. What was going on

downstairs? Was someone banging on the front door? Was that what had awakened her?

She pattered down the stairs and opened the door a crack.

"Oh, Gladell, it's you!" Donna said, opening the door to admit a heavy-set woman wearing a bulky coat, her head wrapped in a coarse wool scarf.

"Who'd ya think it'd be?" asked the woman, setting down a large paper shopping bag and untying her scarf. "I been bangin' on that there door for ten minutes. Thought you was all dead, or somethin'. An' after I near caught my death traipsin' through all that snow."

"We were sound asleep," Donna apologized. "But it was nice of you to come out in this weather, just to clean the house."

"A promise is a promise," Gladell replied as she shut the closet door and picked up the shopping bag. "I told your mother I'd be here every week while she's gone, an' she knows I never go back on my word. Knowed her since before you was born, and she's learned that if there's one thing I am, it's dependable. Now I'm going to change my clothes and get that vacuum cleaner goin'. So tell your sleepyhead brother he'd better get movin'."

Donna raced up the stairs and shook Jimmy's prostrate

figure. "Come on, Jimmy, Gladell's here." Then she ran to put on her clothes.

"Wow," Donna thought as she pulled on her dungarees. "I forgot all about her coming today. It's a good thing I straightened up the kitchen a little last night, or she would have had fits. She's even worse than Mother about putting things away."

"Donna, what's this?" the woman called. Now what, thought Donna, as she slipped into a pair of loafers and rushed downstairs again.

"You know your mother don't allow this bird in the kitchen," Gladell said accusingly. "You get that cage and that bird back where they belong."

Donna did as she was told. "It's warmer out here on the back porch today, birdie," she whispered. "It won't be so bad."

But somehow the dove looked unhappy. Its throat swelled, and it emitted a loud squawk. "I'm sorry, birdie," Donna said softly. "But I know what I'll do for you." She opened the wire door of the cage. "Now you can fly out whenever you want to, and then fly back. I'll keep the kitchen door closed. Gladell has to clean the whole downstairs before she gets out here, and I'll be back before then."

"There." She raised her voice to be heard over the roar of the vacuum cleaner. "I put the cage on the back porch."

Gladell merely nodded and continued working.

"This is one morning I didn't mind getting up," said Miss Dengrove happily as she, Donna, and Jimmy ate their breakfasts. "I can't wait to get outside."

"Me, too," Jimmy agreed. "Can we build a snow fort soon as we're through?"

"First we shovel the walks, m'boy," laughed Marjorie. "I've been snowbound long enough."

Bundled in ski pants, jackets, boots, gloves, and warm hats, they were soon outside, knee-deep in snow.

The bright sun, the cheerful chirping of the sparrows, the calls of boys and girls, the drip of melting snow, seemed to clear away all the grayness of the last few days as quickly as the shovels cleared away the mountains of snow.

"Hey, this pile comes almost to my waist," called Jimmy, manfully struggling with a huge snowdrift.

"Don't get lost in it," called a boy who was picking his way through the snow toward the Parker house.

"Oh, it's Kenny, the paper boy," Donna explained to Miss Dengrove. "I guess he came to collect for last week's newspapers."

"Yes'm," said Kenny. "This sure is a hard way to make a living." He smiled at the teacher.

"I'll get the money to pay him," called Donna from the porch. She shook off as much snow as she could, then opened the door and ran to the kitchen.

"Hey, there," called Gladell after her. "I just finished cleaning that there hall."

"I'll only be a second," said Donna, reaching into the cooky jar and finding the necessary coins. She ran out quickly, leaving Gladell to glare at her.

"Here it is." She handed Kenny the money, with an extra dime that she knew her mother gave him each week for putting the newspaper in the mailbox, instead of throwing it on the porch.

"Where's Jimmy?" she asked as Kenny thanked her and plodded off.

"He just went into the house for some cookies," explained Miss Dengrove.

"Ooh, Gladell will practically shoot him for getting the house dirty again."

Jimmy appeared a few seconds later, however, his mouth and pockets bulging, and seeming none the worse for his encounter with Gladell.

"Back to work," called Miss Dengrove cheerily, and the three began shoveling with renewed vigor. But scarcely had the shovels cleared another foot of the walk when progress was halted again.

"Hey, you!" called Gladell's voice from the porch. "You there!" All three turned and looked at her. "You be Miss Dengrove or somethin'?"

Marjorie's shovel stayed in mid-air. She nodded.

"You be wanted on the telephone." And with a slam of the door, the cleaning woman was gone.

"For me?" queried the teacher. "Now who could that be?"

The conversation lasted long enough for Donna and Jimmy to clear several more feet of the walk.

"It was only my landlady," Miss Dengrove explained when she returned. "She wanted to know when I'm coming for the rest of my clothes."

For a while there were no more interruptions and they worked busily. Then suddenly the front door was flung open, and an obviously irate Gladell called, "You there, you Donna Parker, you get up here this very instant."

"Me?" Donna looked at Marjorie and her brother as if they could bear witness that she had done no wrong. "Why, what happened, Gladell? Did I do anything?"

"*Do* anything?" the woman spluttered as she marched Donna to the kitchen. "She says did she do anything! Look at that!"

She pointed to the kitchen table, on the middle of which sat the white dove.

"Why—why—" Donna stammered. "But how could it—"

"Just wanted a little cool air in here while I was doin' the scrubbin'," Gladell said by way of explanation. "So I opened the door to the back porch and went about my business. And the next thing I know, this devil on wings is flappin' around, back and forth, back and forth, now here, now there, on the cupboards and in the dining room and into the hall closet and all over the place. Don't know how long it's been flyin' around when I didn't even hear it."

"But it can't hurt you," Donna said. "Here, birdie, come on, birdie, did Gladell scare you?" She moved gingerly toward the table.

"I like that!" the woman fumed. "Did *I* scare the bird? How about that bird scarin' me half out o' my wits? I'll tell you, I don't like this at all. First I have to almost break the door down to get in here. Then you and your brother and

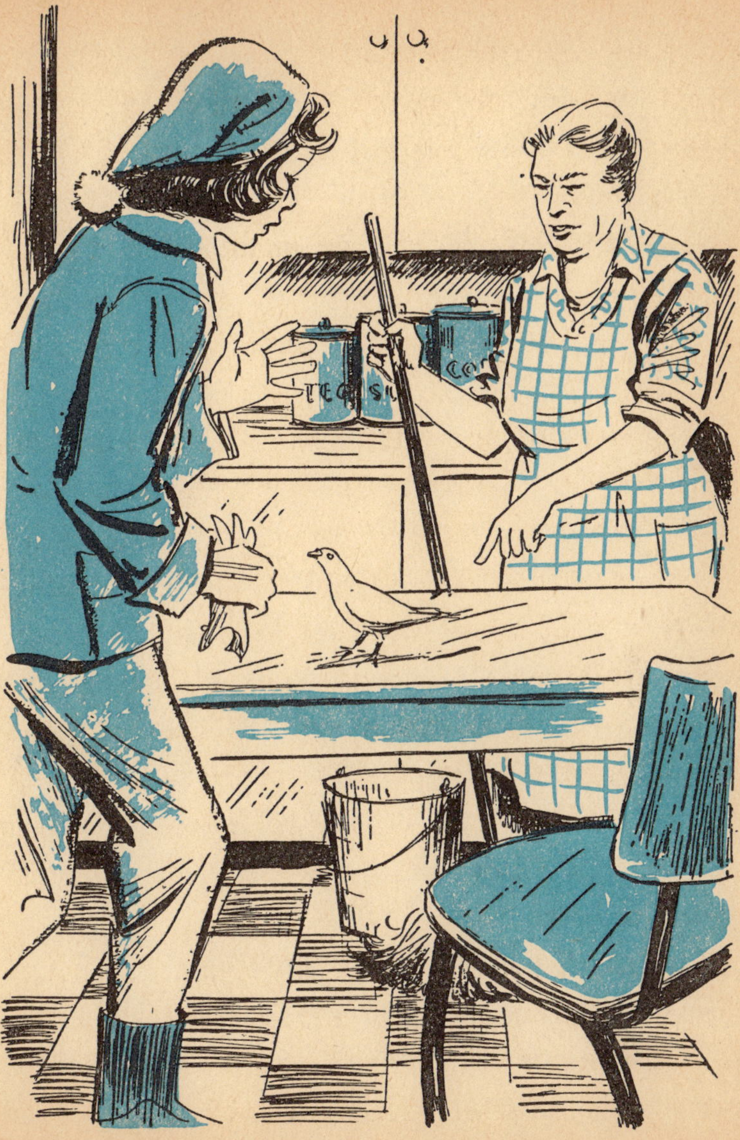

that teacher keep comin' in and out, and interferin' with my work. And now this!" She stomped off, and the girl could hear her mumbling to herself.

Donna reached for the bird, and holding it gently, took it back to its cage. She made sure that both the cage door and the kitchen door were closed, and rejoined the others outside.

"Boy, she was really mad!" Jimmy said, scraping some snow with the back of his shovel.

"It was only because the bird got out of its cage," Donna explained. "But I guess it is annoying. It's much easier for her to clean when we're at school and only Mommy is home."

"I have a wonderful idea," Marjorie suggested. "We've been in the house for so long.... And besides, I hate the thought of disturbing Gladell when we all go in for lunch."

Donna and Jimmy listened expectantly.

"So how would you like to go down to the Sweet Shop and get a hamburger and a milkshake? I think the streets are cleared enough now for me to drive."

"Good! Wonderful!" they chorused.

"And we could make sure the battery in the car doesn't run down," said Jimmy.

Marjorie and Donna laughed. "Of course he's not interested in mere food," Donna smiled. "He's only going because of the car. Are we ready now? I'll go in and get the money."

"No," she added, because Marjorie was beginning to protest. "Mommy said you mustn't spend your own money. There's plenty here. I saw it when I went to get the change to pay Kenny. A five-dollar bill and a one."

She tiptoed inside, determined not to disturb Gladell. There was the cooky jar, with its lid lying on the counter.

"Didn't I put the lid back on the jar?" Donna thought. "That was really careless of me." She put her hand in, then pulled it out again. She took the jar over to the window and looked inside carefully. There were only a few quarters, some dimes, and the dollar bill.

"But I know there was a five-dollar bill there before," she protested. "I just know it." Maybe it was under the lid. No. Could it be someplace else on the counter? No. Had it blown off and landed on the floor? No. Not there either.

"Who's that?" called Gladell.

"Just me," Donna answered. Should she say she was looking for a missing five-dollar bill? She knew the cleaning woman was sensitive about things like that, but of course Gladell didn't have anything to do with the loss. No matter how annoyed she got, she would never . . . .

But who else had been in the house? Jimmy had gone in to get some cookies, but why would he take five dollars? And Marjorie had gone to answer the telephone—oh, really, this was ridiculous.

She would just use her allowance money and say nothing about it. Maybe she had just imagined that the bill was there. After all, she had left the lid off the cooky jar, and that was being careless enough. Or had she? She really couldn't remember whether she had put the top on or not.

And the five-dollar bill? She remembered the way she had had to lift it up to get the coins underneath for Kenny. It must have been there. And it certainly wasn't anywhere around now. Who was responsible?

CHAPTER 8   *Committees and Phone Calls*

Donna ran up the stairs to her room. How much money should she take? She counted the bills in the little purse where she had put her six weeks' allowance, and her heart sank as she realized the dent that would result by withdrawing five dollars.

"Hamburgers and milkshakes won't be nearly that much, though," she thought, tossing her head. "I'll put all the change back. And probably that old five-dollar bill from the cooky jar will turn up in some silly place. Anyhow, I'm certainly not going to worry about it."

She raced down the stairs and out into the bright sunshine.

"We were getting worried," said Marjorie, pulling off her wet gloves. "Was anything wrong, Donna?"

Should she mention the matter to the teacher? How could she, when she wasn't sure of what had happened?

And maybe Marjorie was sensitive, like Gladell, and would feel she was being accused. No, the less said the better.

"She's such a slowpoke," complained Jimmy, saving Donna the necessity of answering. "Come on, I'm hungry."

The drive to the Sweet Shop, though short, was exciting. Apparently all the children were celebrating their release from the three-day confinement and were wallowing in the snow. Forts, houses, queer-looking snowmen, and all sorts of things were being constructed. The driving itself was hazardous, or so it seemed to Donna and Jimmy, and they were constantly pointing out snowbanks and obstructions to Miss Dengrove.

"Wow!" exclaimed Jimmy, as they stopped before a small store with a large plate glass window and blue neon signs. "For a woman driver, you're not so bad, Miss Dengrove. I hope we make it back all right."

"Don't you worry one little bit," Marjorie laughed. "At home I drive over worse roads than that all winter."

"Where's home?" asked Donna, wondering where driving conditions like this would be commonplace.

"Oh—upstate," answered Miss Dengrove vaguely.

And then they were in the Sweet Shop. And there was Ricky, with her back to the door, drinking a coke!

Donna flew to her, covered the red-headed girl's eyes with her hands, and giggled, "Guess who!" But she couldn't wait for Ricky to guess, and removing her hands, slid into the booth beside her friend.

Ricky flung her arms around Donna and then they both started to talk at once.

"Oh, my goodness," Donna said a second later. "I was so excited about seeing you, I just left Miss Dengrove standing at the door with Jimmy. You must come over and meet her, Rick."

Lunch consisted more of chattering than eating, although Donna managed to consume two hamburgers and a large "black and white" milkshake.

Ricky explained that she had come the entire way to the luncheonette on foot. "Because I was so tired staying at home I thought I'd expire," she explained. "Thank goodness I have these high boots, or I would have been soaked to the skin. Did you ever see so much snow?"

It was quickly arranged, after a phone call to Ricky's mother and a consultation with Miss Dengrove, that Ricky would go back to the Parker house.

"Mother says I have to be back before dark, but it's not far from your house to mine. I guess everyone will have the walks shoveled by then anyhow, so I won't mind at all," added Ricky.

The presence of her friend gave Donna's spirits quite a lift.

"Ooh, I'm exhausted," she said happily late that afternoon, as the two girls watched the red sun moving toward the horizon. They sank down on the newly cleared front steps and were silent for a moment.

"But it was so much fun," Ricky giggled. "Remember when Miss Dengrove washed Jimmy's face with snow? And that was a great snowball fight we had. I'm glad they won. She's lots of fun, even though she is a teacher."

Donna nodded. "I knew she would be. We'll have a wonderful time together. She's more like a pal than a mother."

The front door opened, and both girls turned to see Gladell, once again clad in her heavy coat and bright kerchief, standing on the porch.

"I'm ready to leave now," the woman announced.

"I'd better run, too," said Ricky, rising and dusting the back of her ski pants. "The sun's going down awfully fast. See you in school tomorrow, Don."

Gladell continued to stand on the porch as though she

were waiting there for something.

"Her money!" Donna realized. Aloud she said, "I'll get your check, Gladell. It'll only take a minute."

"I'd better make sure I get the one with the right date," Donna thought, "so there's no trouble about that." She examined the checks in the envelope marked "Gladell," selected the proper one, and then thumbtacked the envelope back to the kitchen bulletin board.

"Here it is," she said, as she handed the money to the woman. "Thanks for coming, Gladell. I'm sorry we were such nuisances."

"Oh, well," said the woman, shrugging her shoulders. "Things was nice and quiet this afternoon. See you next week. You're a good girl, Donna."

Donna stared after her, puzzled. She had always felt Gladell was gruff. It certainly was difficult to tell what she was really thinking.

The unaccustomed exercise and fresh air had tired everyone. Luckily the food that Mrs. Parker had left in Mrs. Gray's freezer made dinner preparations a simple matter. The evening meal was a quiet one, and even Jimmy made no protest about going to bed early.

"School tomorrow," thought Donna cozily as she turned

off her bed lamp. "The first time I'll see the gang since Mommy and Daddy left. Wait'll I tell them about the cable from Paris. I wonder what Rome is like."

Her dreams were filled with visions of gay-skirted peasants and handsome Latin men, brilliant flowers, and narrow cobbled streets. But awakening was a different matter, and the morning rush drove from her head all thoughts but those of getting to school on time.

"I never realized I'd be so glad to be back at Summerfield Junior High," Donna said at the end of the school day, as she joined Ricky in the corridor.

"I wouldn't mind staying home one day a week," mused Ricky, "but those three days all in a row were gruesome, weren't they? I really missed seeing the gang."

"Here you are!" panted Anne Franklin, pushing her blond hair off her forehead. "I've been looking for you two ever since the bell rang. Come on with me."

"Now what?" Donna asked.

"George Hart wants to see you. Everybody else is waiting."

"The 'mayor' of the school? Yeeks, this sounds serious!"

Donna could never hear George Hart's name without remembering the exciting school election which George had won, and her own part in it. She had saved the editorial which Joyce Davenport's father had written about it in the *Summerfield Daily Bulletin,* and the clipping was now an important item in her scrapbook. She had loved every minute of the campaign, and even now thrilled to the thought that she had contributed something to an election that was serving as a model for schools all over the country.

Anne led them to a classroom on the second floor, and there they were greeted with various cries.

"At last!" said Jack Kingston. "Can we get started now, George?"

The student head of the school nodded. "Find seats, everyone, and I'll tell you what this is about. We're all here now, I think."

Donna slid into a seat and looked around. Sally Graham, who had been George's opponent in the election, sat near the front of the room. And there were Mary Jefferson, and Steve Collins, and Joyce Davenport, and Bill Blanchard, and even quiet little Tommy Sheridan whose helicopter plans had been the cause of that spy scare just before the newspaper convention. It was flattering to know that she and Ricky were included with the leading members of the class. Whatever did George want with all of them?

"This is our last year at Summerfield Junior High," the boy began. "When we came here, we were children, and when we leave we'll be grown-up."

Donna nodded. It was hard to believe that she had ever been like the little seventh-graders. And soon she and her classmates would be ready for senior high school! Would she ever be as happy there as she was here at junior high?

"—spring dance," George was saying, and there was a whoop from the assembled boys and girls.

"What'd he say?" Donna whispered across the aisle to Ricky. She really must stop this daydreaming.

"He wanted to know if we would like to have a spring dance. He said not all ninth-grade classes had them, but Mr. Greer said that if we wanted to, we could."

"We'd have to ask all the members of the class, wouldn't we?" Bill Blanchard suggested to the group.

George looked around for comment.

"First I think we ought to decide when we'd want to hold it, and what kind it would be, and then ask the class to vote," offered Joyce Davenport.

"Why should we make the decisions? Why not the whole class?" Mary Jefferson asked.

There were various reactions, until finally George Hart

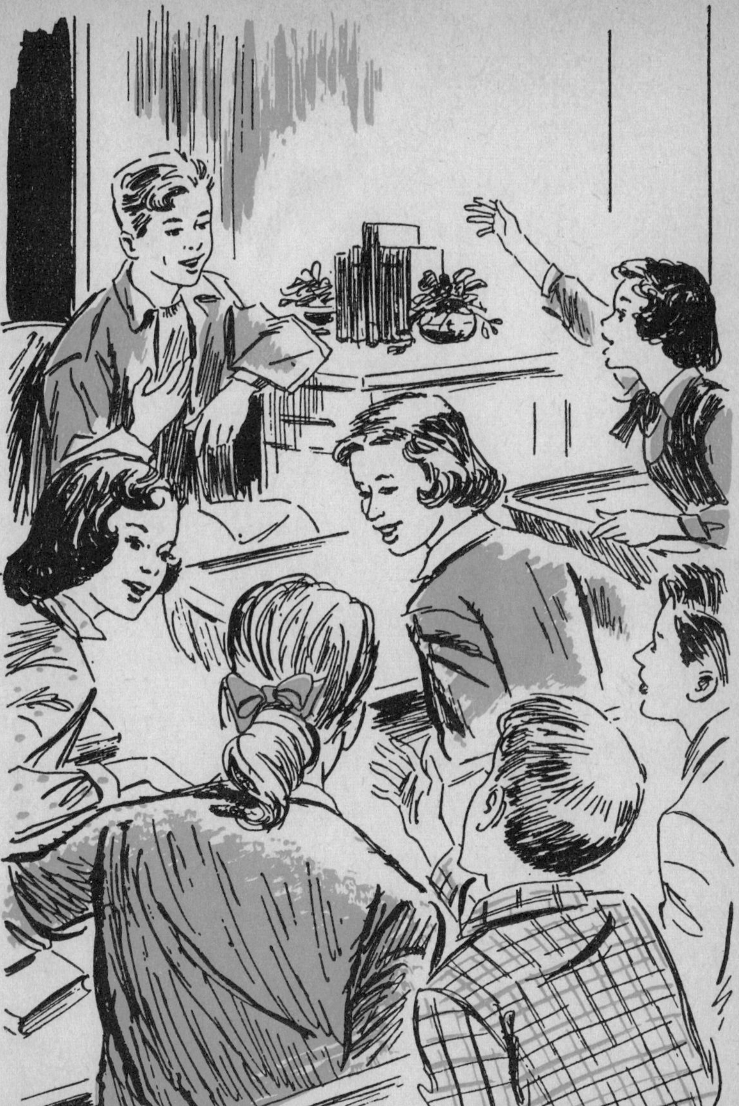

rapped on a desk and called for order.

"I think that if we don't decide some of the things, as Joyce suggested, it would take six weeks to get the whole class to agree even on the date," said George. "Mr. Greer said that we couldn't hold it too late in the term, because we'll have to begin preparations for graduation, and it's the end of March already." As heads nodded, he continued, "Now could we decide when we should have the dance, and whether it should be an afternoon or evening affair?"

It took very little time for the group to come to the conclusion that: first, they would like to have the dance if the majority of the class agreed; second, if it were held just before the Easter vacation, that would give them time to make plans but still allow time for graduation preparations after the holiday; and finally, by unanimous decision, that they wanted the affair in the evening.

"We've accomplished a great deal," said George as they rose to leave. "Since this group seems to work together so well, may I suggest that you all be on the dance committee? We'll try to have the voting done in a few days, during home-room period, and then we'll have another meeting next week."

So she was on the committee! This was really exciting.

There would be so much to do, so many plans to be made. She couldn't wait to tell her—

Donna stopped short. Her mother wasn't home! Here she was, bursting with news, and her mother was off someplace on the other side of the globe.

But there was still Miss Dengrove. Certainly Marjorie would be interested, even if it weren't the same as telling your own mother.

To her dismay, when she arrived home the front door was locked.

"It's a good thing I brought my key," Donna thought as she let herself into the empty house. She knew that Jimmy had been ordered to go to Miss Dengrove's classroom immediately after school each day. "So I won't have to worry about his being on the street," Mrs. Parker had said. "I know Donna has after-school activities, and Miss Dengrove might want to stay late." Amazingly, Jimmy had not protested, especially after Miss Dengrove had promised that he could wash the blackboards each day.

"All alone!" Donna sighed, as she put her books in the usual place on the hall table. "It seems so strange not to find Mommy in the kitchen, or sewing upstairs."

She hung up her coat and headed for the kitchen from

force of habit. Only then did she become conscious of a recurring noise that filled the house.

"My bird!" she thought. "Even during the snowstorm it didn't make this much racket."

She hurried out to the back porch and looked at the dove.

"Something's wrong," she thought. "I don't like the way it looks." The bird sat huddled in a corner of the cage, its tail drooping, feathers ruffled, head cocked to one side, and its usually bright eyes dull and clouded. The croaking came at regular intervals.

"At first you sounded a little like a crow. Now you sound like a full-grown rooster!" Donna thought in consternation. "There must be something terribly wrong for you to look so strange and to make all that noise."

But what could she do? She snapped her fingers at a sudden idea and ran to the telephone.

"The pet shop!" she said aloud. "They ought to know what the trouble is."

The man at the shop was very friendly and asked her a great many questions. Then, to her great disappointment, he admitted that he didn't have the faintest idea what was wrong with the bird.

"The only place that might help you," he suggested, "is a zoo."

"Thank you." Donna put the receiver back with a feeling of helplessness. The nearest zoo she knew was a small one in Byersville, near the camp to which she had gone the summer before. But Byersville meant a long-distance call, and that in turn meant money.

"This gets to be a dreadful headache," Donna thought. "I just spent all that money on lunch at the Sweet Shop yesterday, and I still haven't found the missing five-dollar bill, if there ever was one to begin with. Can I afford to make a long-distance call now?"

Her head swam. Then she shrugged her shoulders. "Something will turn up," she decided. "And I've just got to find out what's the matter with my dove."

It was some minutes before the operator was able to connect her with the zoo, and several more before the head of the bird-and-small-animal department could be located.

"I guess I should have made the call person-to-person," Donna thought, listening to the kitchen clock tick on and on. "But I thought this would be saving money."

Eventually the proper man was found, and he listened to Donna's story.

"I'm surprised that the bird has gotten along as well as it has," the man said when Donna finished. "Doves aren't house birds, you know. I'm glad you have it in a flight cage, and you're right to allow it out several times a day. Be sure to continue doing that."

"There," Donna thought triumphantly. "Wait'll I tell Mommy!"

"The cough, however, worries me," the man continued. "Doves are part of the pigeon family, and all pigeons are likely to get T.B.—tuberculosis, you know. In that case, of course, you'd have to get rid of the bird immediately. Before you do that, though, you could try something for a short while."

"What's that?" Her one pet, and now it was practically lost to her.

"Soak the bird food overnight in a tablespoon of castor oil. Also, get a mixture of charcoal and gravel from your pet shop, and sprinkle it on the floor of the cage for the bird to peck. If there isn't an improvement in a short time, you'll have to get rid of the dove."

Donna felt crushed. Castor oil, charcoal, gravel! Of course she would have to buy them. But goodness knows how much they would cost! Did money always disappear so quickly? She could feel it literally slipping through her fingers.

It was too late to go to the pet store now, though. She would go tomorrow right after school.

The sound of the front door opening brought her thoughts back sharply. "Donna, are you home?" called Miss Dengrove.

"Hey, Sis! Come on in here! Look what we got!" Jimmy cried.

Donna strolled dejectedly into the hall. Miss Dengrove looked up.

"Oh, there you are, Donna. The front door was unlocked, and I assumed you were home. But then I saw that the mail was still in the box, so I wasn't sure."

The mail! She had been so intent on telling Marjorie about the dance committee when she got home that she had forgotten to see if any letters had arrived. What a scatterbrain she was!

Jimmy kept waving an envelope in her face. The bright red and blue stripes around the edge attracted her attention. Air mail!

"It's from Mommy and Daddy!" she cried, seizing the letter eagerly.

"And I got a letter from my mother, too," said Marjorie, holding out an elegant-looking envelope with a return address engraved on the back. "You open yours first, Donna."

CHAPTER 9 *Suspicions*

Donna looked at the postmark on the envelope in her hand.

"Zurich, Switzerland," she read.

"Hey, stop examining it and find out what they wrote," said Jimmy. "I wish Mom would write so's I could read it," he complained.

Jimmy still found printing much easier to read than writing.

"Don't be so impatient," Donna answered. "I have to be careful if you want me to save this beautiful Swiss stamp for you."

"Oh, boy."

Jimmy danced on one foot, then said not a word while Donna tore open the envelope and took out a thin, carefully creased sheet of paper. She unfolded it and read:

Dear Children, and Miss Dengrove, too,

    Just a few lines while we're waiting at the Zurich Airport. The trip across the Atlantic Ocean was delightful, once we got through the storm area. Dinner wasn't served until ten thirty that night because the flight was so bumpy, and then it was time to go to sleep. We awoke over Ireland to a clear blue sky and gorgeous green patches beneath us. We had breakfast in Shannon, and each of us got a sprig of real Irish shamrocks that looked like tiny four-leaf clovers. But they didn't bring us all the good luck we could have hoped for, because after we sent you the cable from Paris we learned that there would be a six-hour delay in our flight.

    Donna turned to Miss Dengrove. "Oh, wasn't that too bad! Then how did they get to Zurich?"

    "If you read it, maybe you'll find out," Jimmy said

impatiently, and Donna continued:

> Luckily, another airplane was going on to Zurich and Rome, and we were able to get on that flight. So here we are now, in this magnificent airport, having had a delicious steak dinner supplied by the airline —

"Wow!" Jimmy interrupted. "Free eats!"

> and we're supposed to get to Rome before midnight tonight. Tomorrow's a holiday, and we leave for India on Tuesday, so goodness knows whether I'll be able to do any shopping in Italy.
>
> How are you all getting along at home? Our thoughts are with you constantly. We can only hope that next time the whole family will be able to make this trip together, for we know you'd love it.
>
> Be good, and don't forget to write.
>
> Love,
> Mother

Donna sighed. There was a moment's silence.

"Now gimme the stamps." Jimmy held out his hand.

His sister dreamily handed the envelope to him. "Gee, Mommy sounds as though they're having a super time. I wonder what they're doing in Rome now." Her mind seemed to be half a world away.

"When you write to your parents, I'll enclose a little note, too," said Miss Dengrove.

The remark snapped Donna back to reality. "Oh, you haven't even opened your letter. Is it something important?"

The teacher deftly slit open the envelope and glanced down the sheet filled with bold handwriting.

"Not another one!" the young woman laughed. "Good old Mumsy!"

Donna looked at Miss Dengrove quizzically, and the teacher laughed again. "My mother is always finding an old school friend, or some long lost relation, wherever anyone goes. I thought I was safe here in Summerfield, but I was wrong. Did you ever hear of a Stacey Cunningham?"

Donna pondered a moment. "Stacey Cunningham? Maybe Mommy or Daddy has, but I've never heard of anybody by that name."

Miss Dengrove consulted the letter again. "Mumsy says

this Mrs. Cunningham is always off on trips someplace, and she hasn't seen her for years and years. They went to Miss Fordham's School together. Here—maybe this will help.

> I'm sure dear Stacy will be delighted to meet you—if I know her she'll be amazed that I have a daughter who's old enough to be a teacher. Poor thing, she's had a lonely life ever since her husband died. No children, and that huge house, and more money than she knows what to do with. She hates to admit to the passing of the years, and I'm sure some young lively company will do her good. The newspaper reports

say she'll be back in Summerfield in a few days, so do be a good girl and call her.

"I wonder . . ." Donna mused. "I just wonder if that could be Mrs. John Q. X. Cunningham. Everything seems to fit—the big house, and the traveling, and her husband being dead."

"Then you do know something about her, Donna?"

"Not much—if it's the same one. The estate is out beyond Summerfield, and it's all hidden from the road, so I have no idea what it's like. And I've never seen Mrs. Cunningham. She's away most of the time, I've heard, and has nothing to do with the people in Summerfield. Oh, isn't this exciting?"

Miss Dengrove's expression was glum. "Don't be too sure, Donna. Mumsy has dragged me around to so many weird characters who are her friends, that I always approach a new one with fear and trembling."

"Suppose you get invited out there? Wouldn't that be super, Margie?"

"You'd come too, of course. I'd want you for protection,

if for no other reason. You never know what's going to happen when you meet one of Mumsy's old school friends."

Donna smiled. Miss Dengrove must be teasing: She didn't sound really frightened at all. Certainly Mrs. Cunningham wouldn't bite!

But if Donna could have foreseen what difficulties she and her friends would get into, because of her future meeting with the wealthy widow, she might have had some of Marjorie Dengrove's hesitancy.

Things seemed to go almost too smoothly for the next few days. At school, the newspaper was doing well now that Joyce Davenport was back and in charge. Since Miss Fischer, the teacher who had been the sponsor, had left to marry Donna's uncle and to move to California, Mr. Greer himself was supervising the staff. Donna was relieved not to feel the full responsibility for the *Summerfield Sum-It-Up,* to return to her original job as assistant editor, and to leave the major share of running the newspaper to Joyce.

As George Hart had predicted, voting about the ninth-grade spring dance was completed quickly, and to the delight of the dance committee almost everyone in the class wanted an evening affair.

At home, too, things seemed to be falling into a routine. Everyone was co-operating in keeping the house in fairly orderly condition, and Mrs. Gray, like the good neighbor she was, helped to keep things running smoothly. It was comforting, when Donna went over each evening to get food from the freezer, to know that Mrs. Gray was there in case of trouble. Luckily, Donna thought, she had not needed her for anything so far, and she was sure that Mrs. Gray would tell her mother how grown-up Donna had been.

There seemed to be only two minor disturbances on the horizon. One was that since the letter from Zurich, Donna had received no word from her parents. The other—and she did not know whether or not she should mention this in her next letter to her mother—was that Jimmy was coming home from school later and later each day, and often without Miss Dengrove.

Marjorie had not seemed disturbed by this. "It's tryout time for the baseball team, Donna and you know how much the team means to Jimmy," she had said when Donna had gotten up courage to mention the subject. "Besides, Mr. Curtin is in charge, and I'm sure he takes good care of the boys."

"I guess she's right," Donna thought, "and I'm turning out to be a worry wart, but I'd feel better if Mother agreed. After all, she did say that Jimmy was to come home with Miss Dengrove every day. I do wish we'd get a letter from them soon."

Donna was doomed to disappointment the next day too, however. For although there was a large collection of mail in the letter box when she arrived home from school, most of it consisted of ads and bills. And a large, interesting-looking cardboard package contained nothing more exciting than a book called *The Behavior of Children*.

"Something else for Mommy's study group, I guess," thought Donna, as she placed the book on the kitchen table and threw the cardboard wrapping into the large wastebasket near the sink. "But not a word from Mommy or Daddy. Well, I guess I'd better write to them again, anyhow. I guess they're in Madras by now."

The letter took only a few minutes to compose, including everything that Donna thought would interest her parents about the smooth running of the house, the dance committee at school, and the news about Mrs. John Q. X. Cunningham. "Oh, and I'll tell them my dove is much better now. I'm sure they'll be interested in hearing about that—

at least Daddy will be interested."

She laid her pen on the table. "Come to think of it, it's awfully quiet on the back porch. I'd better see if the bird is really all right."

The food and medicine that Donna had gotten from the pet shop had seemed to help the bird's cough, and she had begun to hope that all the trouble had stemmed from a simple cold.

Even to Donna, the dove now looked fine. Its eyes were bright again, its feathers unruffled. "I'm sure it's all right now," she thought with relief. Then, looking at its now-gray feathers, "Putting charcoal in the cage may have helped its cough, but it certainly didn't do much toward keeping it clean. My white dove looks as though it has been bathing in coal dust. I wonder if you can wash a bird with soap and water."

She slid the wire door up and reached in for the dove. Stroking its feathers and cooing softly, she carried it into the kitchen and set it on the table. "Maybe when it gets to know me well enough, it'll learn to do tricks," Donna thought, remembering her experience in animal training during the snow storm. Although the bird still liked to scratch papers, it seemed far removed from jumping

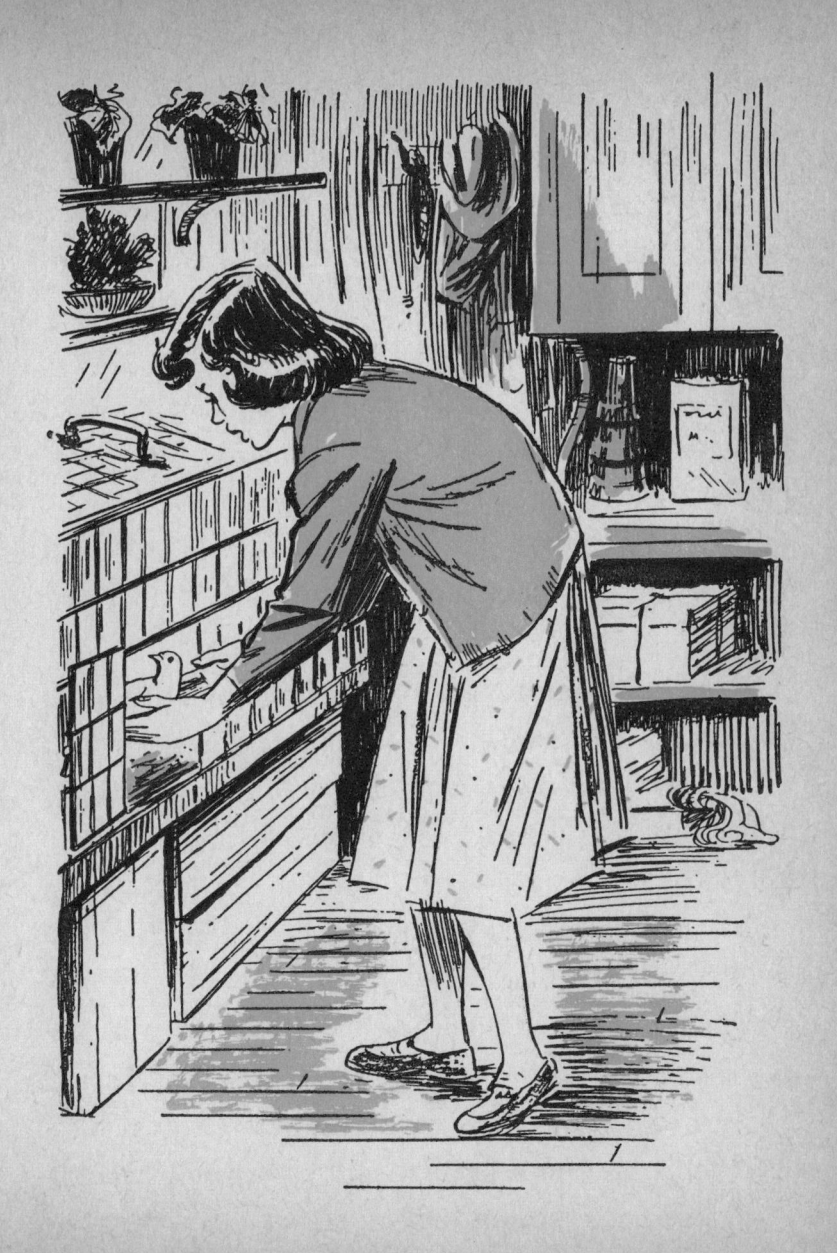

through hoops or obeying any orders at all.

"Now don't tear up the letter I just wrote," Donna warned, as she snatched the paper away before the bird's claws could get to it. "You just sit there.

"I'd better put Mommy's new book away, too." She glanced idly through the pages, and her eye was caught by a section that said "The Eight-Year-Old." "Sa-ay, this man might be writing about Jimmy," she thought, as she read that eight-year-olds have to be reminded to wash their hands, often bolt their food, usually enjoy team sports like baseball, and love to play "bombing" and war games.

"That's Jimmy all right," she thought, turning to the next page. Then she gasped.

" 'Eight-year-olds are beginning to learn what money can buy,' " she read aloud. " 'Sometimes they may even help themselves to the household funds. They often use this money not for themselves, but to treat their friends.' "

She closed the book, and her eyes went to the cooky jar. Since the day they had gone to the Sweet Shop, she had used her allowance money only for school. Jimmy, of course, had his lunch tickets. And so far they hadn't had to buy anything at the store, though they were beginning to run low on bread now. That meant that the dollar bill and the change should still be in the cooky jar—unless someone had been helping himself.

Donna walked thoughtfully to the counter and raised the lid of the jar. She breathed a sigh of relief. Everything was accounted for.

Except, of course, that first five-dollar bill. Had she really imagined it? Or had Jimmy helped himself and spent it on his friends?

The front door slammed, and Miss Dengrove called, "Donna?" The teacher came directly into the kitchen.

"I thought I heard you back here," the young woman said. "Oh, have you been writing to your folks?"

Donna nodded and turned back to the cooky jar. "I was just going to get some money for stamps."

"Good," agreed Miss Dengrove. "I wrote a little note today, too. Would you mind enclosing it with your letter? And I wrote to my mother, too, telling her that Mrs. Cunningham hasn't arrived yet. Would you mail that for me, too, Donna?" Marjorie laid the envelope and a sheet of paper on the kitchen table, and went to hang her coat in the hall closet.

"Gee, she didn't even offer to pay for the stamps," thought Donna, lifting the lid off the cooky jar again.

Just then she heard behind her the sound of paper being scratched.

"Oh, that dreadful bird! It's gotten to the letters," she thought and turned to rescue the papers. But the bird, startled by her sudden movement, flew off to the top of the cupboard, which by now seemed to be its favorite resting place.

Donna, in turn startled by the bird, dropped the lid of the cooky jar on the floor, where it fell with a loud crash and broke into a dozen pieces.

"Now you just stay up there, you old bird," she said, pointing a warning finger at the dove.

"Did something happen?" Miss Dengrove called. And then, without waiting for an answer, "You'd better go quickly, Donna, if you want to get that air-mail stamp before the post office closes."

"You'd think she'd at least have offered to pick up the broken lid," Donna thought in chagrin as she hurried down the street. "Or she could have said she'd drive me to the post office. After all, it's our car."

Her annoyance was lessened somewhat when the letters were mailed. And she completely forgot any feelings toward Marjorie on her arrival home. For there, standing on the front porch, was a young man in a blue uniform and a messenger's cap.

"Oh, no, not another telegram!" thought Donna in dismay.

"Special-delivery letter, miss," said the young man as she came up the front steps. "I was just going to ring the doorbell."

"From Mommy and Daddy!" Donna cried, rushing into the house and tearing open the envelope.

She read silently for a moment, nodding her head and smiling a little. Then she clapped her hand to her forehead and groaned, "Oh, no!"

Miss Dengrove leaned over the banister in the upstairs hall. "Something wrong, Donna?"

Donna sank down on the bottom step. "Oh, listen to this, Marjorie. It's just gruesome!

And when I looked down in my lap again my purse was gone; it must have dropped out of the car when I opened the door to take some pictures of the Roman Forum. Not that there was much money in it—

but it had my passport and my health certificate, with the record of those dreadful shots I had to take. Poor Daddy has spent half the day at the nearby police station, trying with his little bit of Italian to tell them what happened, and filling out all sorts of papers. If it isn't found, I guess I shall just have to come home. Wouldn't that be a strange ending to my trip abroad?

"Poor Mommy!" Slowly Donna folded the letter and put it on the hall table. "And she looked forward so much to going to India. Do you think there's any chance of the purse being returned, Marjorie?"

"I'm sure everything will work out," Marjorie replied, "but I'm awfully sorry it happened."

"So'm I," Donna agreed. But in the back of her mind there were several other thoughts. So her mother could lose her things, too, and important things at that! Here she had been blaming herself, feeling terribly guilty about the five dollars that was missing. But that wasn't nearly so dreadful as losing a precious passport.

Five dollars! Goodness, she had better remind Marjorie about cashing a check, since there was so little money left. And thinking about the cooky jar, she had better pick up the pieces that were still lying on the kitchen floor.

As she moved toward the kitchen the telephone rang. "Should I answer it?" Jimmy called.

"No!" And to herself she thought, "I didn't even know he was home yet."

"It's the telegraph office again," she explained to Jimmy. "I think they have another cable from Mommy. Oh, I hope she found her passport."

"She what?" Jimmy looked at his sister as though she were talking utter nonsense.

"Never mind," she whispered. " 'Everything fine,' " she repeated after the operator. " 'Passport returned. Proceeding India immediately.' Oh, that's wonderful."

She hung up and sank into a kitchen chair. "Such excitement," she said. "Well, I'm glad that's settled." Then she turned to her brother, remembering all of her own worries now that those of her parents were solved.

"So you finally decided to come home, Jimmy. Did you

come in the back way, after all that Mommy has told you? And why that look on your face? Were you climbing over fences again?"

Jimmy's expression was one of proper indignation. "I did not!" he protested. "Not even one fence. All I did was—was—"

"Out with it!"

Jimmy backed away. "I just put your dirty old bird back in the cage!"

"You—touched—my—bird!" His sister advanced menacingly.

"Well, it was flyin' all around the kitchen, an' I couldn't even open the cupboard to get some cookies. All I did was put it back."

Donna took a quick look on the back porch, where the bird seemed to be sleeping in a corner of the cage. She decided to forgive Jimmy this time.

"Anyhow," he went on, feeling that he had better take the offensive, "who broke the lid to the cooky jar?"

Donna looked at him, startled. She had almost forgotten why she had come into the kitchen.

"That was an accident. I'm cleaning it up now."

She stooped to pick up the pieces, and Jimmy sat down

at the kitchen table. What was the matter with him? thought Donna. He certainly was acting awfully strange. Had that queer troubled expression on his face merely been because he had touched her bird?

A sentence flashed into her mind—*Eight-year-olds are beginning to learn*—she stood up quickly and looked in the cooky jar— *what money can buy*. The dollar bill was gone!

"Jimmy, Jimmy, Jimmy," she said softly. He looked up at her. Were his eyes the least bit tearful looking? Could it be that he was sorry for what he had done?

"Let me have it, Jimmy," she said, holding out her hand. The boy looked at her, seeming not to hear.

"The dollar," she said a little louder. "Give it back."

"What're you talkin' about? You goin' daffy or somethin'?" he asked in disgust, moving away from the table.

"I want the dollar bill you just took from the cooky jar."

"What would I do with a dollar bill? You think I need to buy lipsticks or some crazy junk for my hair, like dopey girls?"

His reply was so sincere that Donna was dumbfounded.

"Jimmy, listen to me," she said in a tone so grave he gave her his full attention. "Did you or did you not take any money out of the cooky jar, now, or ever?"

She watched his face carefully. His eyes looked deep into hers.

"I—did—not!" he stated emphatically and turned his pockets inside out to prove his statement. Then he turned and walked upstairs, dragging his feet.

Donna stared after him. It was obvious that he was telling the truth.

But the only other person in the house was Miss Dengrove. Donna bit her knuckles.

Miss Dengrove was the person her mother had left in charge. She was a responsible person, a teacher. True, she sometimes didn't do things the way her mother did. True, she left dirty dishes in the sink, and didn't seem to care when Jimmy came home late.

But good gracious, this was just what she, Donna, had wanted, wasn't it? Somebody who didn't scold and nag about stupid little things all the time?

And wasn't it silly for these very things to look suspicious, not quite the way a responsible person would act, just because some money was missing?

She chewed on her knuckles. Or was it silly? After all— who else had been in the house?

CHAPTER 10 *Mrs. Cunningham*

"But I'm sure Marjorie must have plenty of her own money," Donna said thoughtfully to Ricky West as they walked home from school together the next day. The morning walk had been too rushed for the girls to finish discussing the matter. "And it's not the sort of thing you can talk about over the phone," Donna had said in a troubled voice.

"Have you noticed those gorgeous cashmere sweaters she wears to school?" Ricky asked now. "Why, they cost a fortune."

"She must come from a wealthy family," Donna continued. "You should see her mother's fancy engraved writing paper. And Mrs. Dengrove went to that elegant Miss Fordham's School in New England. And Marjorie wouldn't even let my mother pay her for staying with us

—she said that it would be so nice to live in a real home again that money didn't matter."

Ricky stopped and turned to face her friend. "Maybe that's it, Don! Maybe now she's sorry she isn't getting paid and decided to help herself to the money that's there. Why don't you ask her?"

The dark-haired girl frowned. "Oh, I couldn't do that. Can't you just see me facing her with a stern look"—she giggled in spite of herself—"pointing a finger at her and saying, 'Pardon me, Miss Dengrove, but will you tell me why you've been helping yourself to the money in the cooky jar and getting me so worried?'"

Ricky nodded. "I guess it does seem silly, over just a few dollars. After all, she may have a perfectly good reason for taking the money, though it does seem strange that she wouldn't say anything about it to you. Unless she's a—a klep—klepto—you know, a person who takes things just for the sake of taking them and not for any real purpose."

"Oh, I know that word you mean. It's like a disease, or a form of insanity. Klepto—wait a minute—kleptomania. Oh, Ricky, you don't think Miss Dengrove is a kleptomaniac, do you?"

"It's possible, Donna. Sometimes it's years before you

find out things like that about people. You know, it's her first teaching job, and nobody in town knows her very well yet. Although I guess the Board of Education had to get some references about her."

"I won't even think such a thing, Ricky." Then she paused. "It's—it's not dangerous, is it?"

The other girl considered a moment. "I don't think so. But maybe we could find out from a library book or something. I'll try to look it up. In the meantime, you'd better check and see whether anything else is missing."

The two girls paused at the bottom step of the Parker house.

"Want to come in a minute, Rick?" Donna asked. It was only a halfhearted invitation.

Ricky shook her head. "Yeeks, Don!" she exclaimed suddenly, almost dropping her armload of books. "I almost forgot the most important thing. Mother asked me to invite you to dinner for tomorrow night. Can you come?"

"I'll have to check with Marjorie," Donna said forlornly, wondering whether she should leave her little brother with someone she knew so little about.

But it would be good to get away from the house for a while. Meals were getting boring at home, too, in spite of all the varied menus her mother had prepared. Somehow dinner tasted better when her mother was in charge.

"I—I think it'll be all right, Rick." Her face brightened. "And I'd really love to come. We have a dance committee meeting after school, so I'd probably be going home late anyhow."

Miss Dengrove seemed quite agreeable when Donna spoke to her about the dinner invitation. "I did want to go to the bank with you tomorrow to cash a check, Donna, but I guess it can wait a day or so. We have a lot of shopping to do, you know."

"Should I ask her about the money now?" thought Donna. But looking at Marjorie, busy marking test papers for her class, all her fears seemed to collapse. How could a pretty, sweet young woman, who looked so studious wearing her horn-rimmed glasses, possibly be a suspicious character?

"It's just that crazy Ricky," Donna thought as she went to her own room. "She goes off on these wild notions and I go right along with her."

Then she paused and walked to the mirror over her bureau. "I shouldn't blame her, though. It's my own fault that I'm so easily swayed. When will I ever learn not to be carried along so completely by other people's ideas?"

She smiled at the image in the mirror. Then she frowned. Had she imagined it, or had the dark-haired reflection really refused to smile back, as though it knew something she didn't? A shudder passed through her. Would this shortcoming of hers that seemed so minor, this wanting to be one of the gang, get her into trouble one day? Was that what the girl in the mirror was trying to tell her?

It was lucky she hadn't said anything to Marjorie about the money. Ricky didn't realize what a nice person Miss Dengrove really was. Tomorrow at Ricky's house she would have to tell her not to get any more of those wild ideas about kleptomaniacs. There must be a much simpler solution.

But somehow the subject was never raised at dinner the next night. There was the afternoon's dance committee meeting to discuss, for one thing.

"I'm so glad we're both on the decorating committee, Don," Ricky said on the way to the West house. "We've got to make this a real super affair, one that the school will never forget."

"Why?" Donna asked, remembering her resolution of the night before to make her own decisions.

"Because"—Ricky looked astounded—"why, just because, Donna. Don't you have any class spirit?" Her voice took on the dreamy quality that meant she was miles away. "It'll be the end of April, and all the spring flowers will be blooming. Maybe we can make the gym look like a garden—you know, decorate it with millions of daffodils and tulips—"

"It sounds like a debutante's coming-out party," Donna said, hoping to bring her friend back to earth.

"That's it, Don, exactly," Ricky seemed delighted that the other girl had caught the feeling. "Only of course at a coming-out party there would be real imported orchids all over the place, not little old tulips."

"Well, we'll probably have to be content with potted palms," Donna smiled. "I don't know where you'd get thousands of tulips, let alone orchids."

Then, as they went up to Ricky's bedroom and laid their schoolbooks down, the red-haired girl said suddenly, "What're you going to wear, Don? To the dance, I mean."

"Wear?" Donna was startled. "I never thought about it. My white dress that Uncle Roger gave me, the one I wore in New York, I guess."

Ricky frowned. "But that's practically a formal, Donna.

Don't you think it's too dressed up for a small town like Summerfield? I mean, none of the other girls . . . ." She didn't finish the sentence.

"They aren't? Well, it's almost a month away. I guess Mommy could make—" Donna clapped her hand over her mouth. "Yeeks! I keep forgetting that my mother isn't here. All I've got are sweaters and skirts and blouses and that tired old brown jumper. Oh, Ricky," and it was almost a wail, "oh, what'll I do?"

Ricky, too, looked disturbed. "I'm going to wear that green chambray that I've only worn once. None of the gang has seen it. It's got a low neck in front and some rhinestone buttons. And I thought I'd wear my pearls. It's dressy, but not too much. But, gee, Donna—"

Donna nodded, scarcely hearing her friend. Why did her mother have to be away now, of all times? She certainly didn't have enough money to buy a new dress.

"I know!" Ricky snapped her fingers. "A friend of my mother's just sent me a rose taffeta dress that was hardly worn by her daughter. I haven't even tried it on, because of course I have the chambray. Let's see how it looks on you."

She raced to a hall closet and came back with a dress over her arm. "See, it's really very simple. Just a full skirt and a plain top, and these little puffed sleeves. Come on, Don, try it."

Reluctantly Donna removed her skirt and blouse and slipped the taffeta dress over her head.

"Oh, Don!" Ricky clapped her hands. "It's just gorgeous. And it fits you absolutely perfectly." She dragged Donna over to the full-length mirror.

The dark-haired girl looked and then dimpled. "It's not bad, is it, Rick? The color is really awfully becoming, and it does fit well, doesn't it?" She twirled and felt her heart give a little jump as the skirt belled out around her. "With a couple of petticoats—"

"Let's show Mother." Ricky grabbed her hands, and they flew down the stairs.

"Of course she may wear it," Mrs. West said when the situation was explained. Then she peered at the dress more closely. "I do think it has a couple of spots, though. Let me have it, and I'll send it to the cleaners. It'll be back in ample time, so don't worry, Donna."

And though Donna protested, and wanted to pay for the cleaning, Mrs. West would hear nothing of it.

Donna walked home that evening as though she were floating on air. "Ricky is certainly a good friend," she

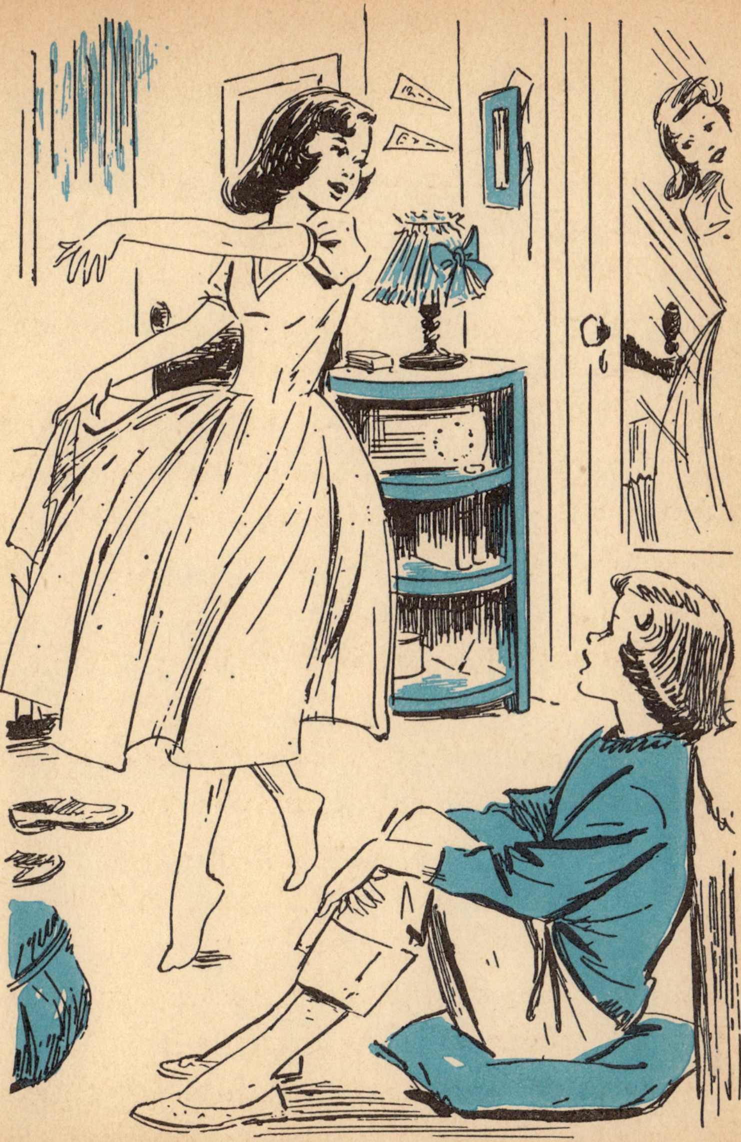

thought. "Now I don't have to worry about a dress for the dance. And dinner was wonderful. It was so good getting out of the house. I'll bet Marjorie must be as bored as I was."

To Donna's surprise, however, Marjorie greeted her with a shout.

"Wait'll I tell you what happened," the teacher cried. "Oh, you'll love this, Donna."

"It must be exciting, to make you look like that," Donna replied, hanging her coat in the hall closet. "Wouldn't you know that the minute I leave something happens?"

"I called Mrs. Cunningham on the phone, and this time she was home. Mumsy must have written to her, too, because she knew all about me. She invited me to come to visit Saturday afternoon and to stay for dinner."

"That's wonderful, Marjorie." Donna squeezed Miss Dengrove's hand. Poor thing, she was probably as happy to get away from the Parker house as Donna had been tonight.

"But that isn't all," the teacher continued. "When I told her that I was staying here, she insisted that I bring you and Jimmy along."

Donna's eyes widened. "Oh!" she gasped. "How wonderful! How will I ever wait until Saturday?"

"Now hold on a minute," Marjorie protested. "Don't get too excited. I told you about Mumsy's queer friends. Mrs. Cunningham may take a little getting used to."

Saturday dawned clear and balmy, which only made matters worse, for Jimmy protested again and again at missing his baseball practice session.

"Why couldn't it have rained?" Donna thought as they drove in the Parker car to the outskirts of town and turned down a narrow road. At last they entered a driveway almost overgrown with large bushes. Jimmy was still pouting on the back seat, mumbling about wasting a day like this when it was so important that he be playing ball.

"Oh, stop grumbling," Donna flung over her shoulder. "One day less of batting that stupid ball around won't make a bit of difference. And remember, you'd better be on your company manners. Yeeks!"

Jimmy shot straight up in his seat. "Now what?"

"Look at that house!" Donna nudged Miss Dengrove.

"Lovely, isn't it?" Miss Dengrove said, slowing the car down.

"And so big!" Donna exclaimed. "Those beautiful white columns, and all that red brick. It's a real colonial mansion, isn't it? And you can't even see it from the road."

They parked at one side of the circular driveway and walked up to the house. A liveried servant answered their ring and said, "You must be Miss Dengrove. Mrs. Cunningham said will you please wait on the sun porch. She'll be down in a few minutes."

He led them through a magnificent entrance hall, complete with circular staircase and marble floor, and past a maze of other rooms out to a large porch enclosed by huge windows and furnished with comfortable chairs, sofas, and small tables.

When the servant had left them, Donna tiptoed over to Marjorie. "Yeeks!" she whispered. "I never knew there were houses like this except in the movies. Wait'll I tell the gang what's right here in Summerfield!"

"You don't have to whisper," said Marjorie smilingly, sinking into a low chair. Jimmy sat himself down in one corner of a large sofa, put his hands deep in his pockets, and wore his most disgusted expression.

"Isn't it just gorgeous?" Donna stared around her. "Imagine really living in a place like this."

"So you like it, do you?" said a husky voice at the doorway to the room. Donna turned and almost tripped over a coffee table.

There, framed in the archway, stood a woman whose age she could not begin to guess, with the brightest orange hair she had ever seen. From her ears hung huge gold circlets, and on her arms were dozens of bracelets, each loaded with charms. She was wearing a high-necked scarlet blouse and green velvet slacks. On her feet were green slippers covered with sequins, with toes that turned up "like the slippers in the pictures of the Arabian Nights," Donna thought. She was too stunned to move.

As the woman came into the room, Marjorie rose. "So you're Marjorie Dengrove," the woman said. "And this must be the little girl you're taking care of. How sweet!"

Donna gulped. "She's—she's wearing false eyelashes," she thought. "Whew! Wait'll I tell Ricky!" She caught Marjorie's eye. So this was one of her mother's "peculiar" friends. Did she imagine it, or had Marjorie winked at her ever so slightly?

"How—how do you do?" she blurted, but Mrs. Cunningham was already sweeping across the room to Jimmy, who seemed to be trying to disappear into a corner of the couch.

"What a sweet, sweet little boy. Come here and tell Aunt Stacey your name."

"James Parker," he mumbled.

"What a lovely name! And I'm going to call you Jamesie."

"Yeeks!" Donna thought. "Jamesie! Of all things!"

Mrs. Cunningham sat down and pulled a small box out of the pocket of her slacks. "How nice that all of you could come. Marjorie, darling, you must tell me all about your dear little mother." She opened the box and waved it around. "Smoke, anyone?" Then, not waiting for an answer, she took out what looked like a long pencil-thin cigar and lit it.

"Yeeks!" Donna thought again, her mouth half-open. What would happen next?

"Would you all like a cup of tea, or a drink of something?" Mrs. Cunningham asked, ringing a bell on the table beside her. When the servant who had shown them in appeared again, Mrs. Cunningham said, "Foster, do take these children out to Cook and keep them happy. And bring us a tea tray. Miss Dengrove and I have so much to talk about."

"Certainly, madam." The butler bowed.

As Donna rose to leave, Marjorie started to speak. Then she stopped, smiled weakly at Donna, and half shrugged her shoulders as though to say, "Didn't I tell you?"

"She might have said something about wanting me to stay," Donna thought. "After all, it's pretty discouraging to be put in the same class with Jimmy and sent out of the room."

But as the butler led them through the various rooms, Donna became so interested she forgot to be upset.

"I'd get lost, living in a house this big," she whispered to Jimmy who was dragging behind her.

When they reached the huge kitchen, the butler turned to them. "Now what would you care to have? Should Cook make some little sandwiches, or would you prefer cake?"

"Cake," said Jimmy promptly. He had strolled over to a counter and was inspecting a large jar which stood on a little chromium counter. "Hey, can you make milkshakes in this thing?"

"Indeed, yes," said Foster. "We'll be happy to make one for you—that is, if we happen to have some milk. Madam isn't much of a milk-drinker."

"I'll bet she isn't," Donna thought. "Anyone who dresses in an outfit like that probably drinks nothing but champagne."

The milkshake and chocolate cake put Jimmy in a much

happier frame of mind. And when Foster suggested that Donna explore the house, she too was delighted.

"I hope I can find my way back," she thought, after having investigated the huge living room, a large formal dining room, a smaller, informal dining room, a library, a wood-paneled room hung with stuffed animal heads, and another room "that must be the study, because how many living rooms can you have?"

The upstairs was even more fascinating. She lost track of the number of bedrooms, because each one seemed to be a small apartment, complete with separate bath, dressing room, and sitting room.

"Let's see," she tried to remember. "There was the pink bedroom with the flowered rug, and the brown bedroom where everything was decorated with diamond shapes, and the green bedroom that had the purple and gold dressing room, and—oh, I give up!"

She tiptoed downstairs and after a few false turns found her way back to the kitchen. But Jimmy was no longer there.

"Foster took him down to the swimming pool," the cook explained. "There's no water in it, but the boy said he wanted to see it anyhow. I can't imagine why."

She gave Donna directions for getting there and showed her the back door.

"Over this hill and past the formal gardens," Donna repeated. Goodness, who would ever believe her when she told them all this? And there, below her, was what must be the swimming pool, as big as the one at the Summerfield Recreation Center.

"And probably nobody ever uses it," she thought. "What a waste!"

"Hey, Sis!" Jimmy's voice came from a clearing past the pool. "Come on over here."

Foster still was with her brother. "I was just taking him to the greenhouse, miss. Would you like to come along?"

Donna nodded.

"Foster said he'd show me a new pitch," Jimmy bubbled. "Didja know he has a brother who used to work for the Yankees?"

"He never played ball, Jimmy. He was just the manager's assistant," Foster reminded him.

"But he knew all the players, didn't he?"

The man nodded. "Here's the greenhouse," he said, pointing to a small building made entirely of glass. "I wonder where Mike is."

"Mike's the gardener," Jimmy explained to his sister. Apparently he was now very much at home here.

Donna was amazed at the rows and rows of plants and brilliantly colored flowers arranged in flowerpots on tables. She listened while Foster explained how the glass house was kept at an even temperature, and how Mike was able to raise enough flowers to keep the house supplied all year round.

"Mrs. Cunningham loves flowers, and Mike raises all sorts of fancy varieties, including some very special ones," he said. "When we have too many for the house, Madam sends them to hospitals and orphanages, and she loves to give them to all her friends."

Something clicked in Donna's mind. All these wonderful flowers— No, she wouldn't even think of it. If Ricky were here, she would probably nudge her into it. She could almost hear Ricky saying, "But, Donna, the dance—"

After all, Donna reasoned, Mrs. Cunningham could hardly be considered a friend of hers, and certainly she wasn't someone you could ask for favors. She wasn't even really a friend of Marjorie's.

At dinner, it was true, Mrs. Cunningham was most cordial and wanted to hear all about Donna's school and her

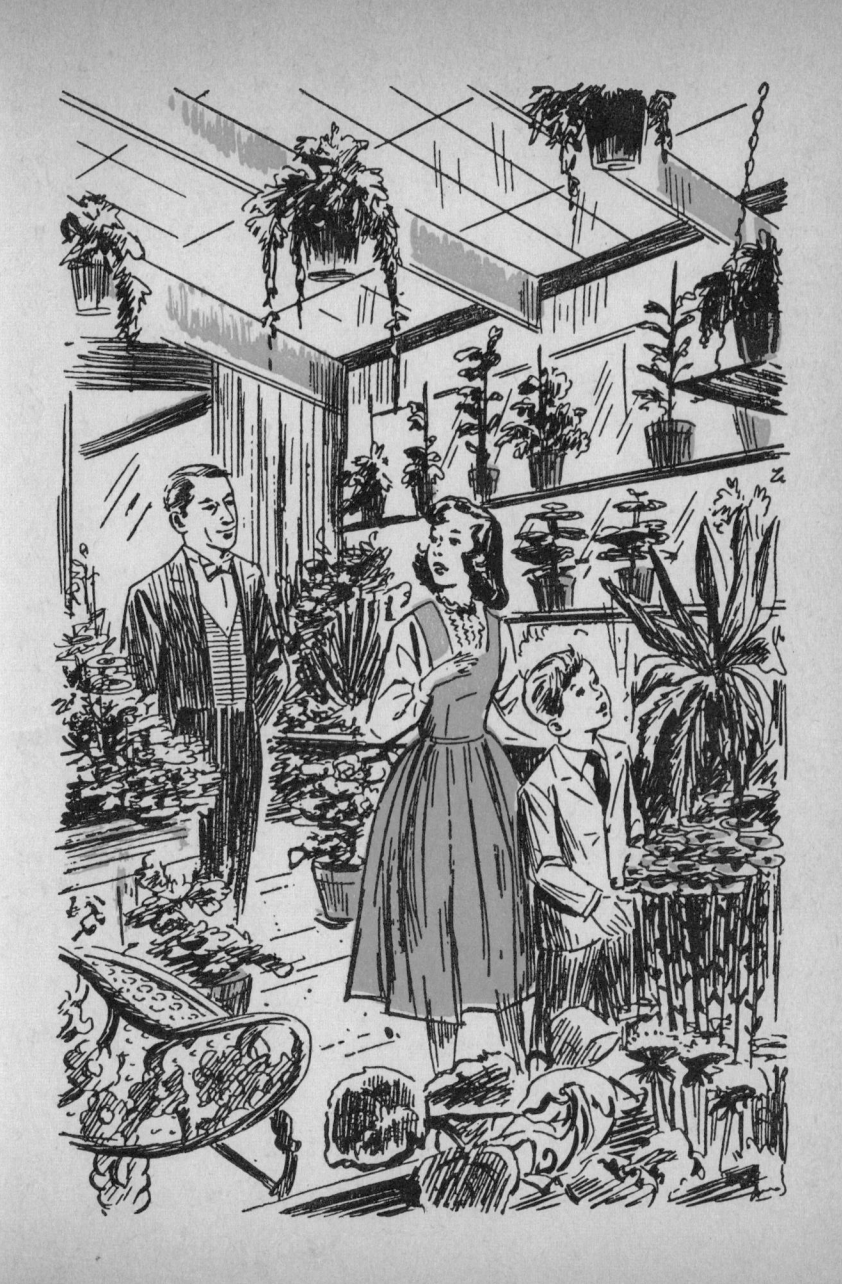

friends. Donna was almost tempted to mention the spring dance.

"So your parents are in India." Mrs. Cunningham leaned forward. "I do hope they get to meet the Maharani of Madras. Such a charming person. I'll never forget that day at the beach. The Bay of Bengal is so blue, you know, and although the Madrasi say there are sharks in the waters, we were never bothered by them. The Maharani was wearing the sweetest little gold-embroidered sari that day, and she just went swimming, sari and all. How she didn't drown with all that business draped around her, I'll never know."

Mrs. Cunningham babbled on, about her travels throughout the East, and the wonderful climate in Ceylon "where you can get the most magnificent star sapphires for practically nothing," and the valley of Kashmir where she had spent the summer on a houseboat, and Hong Kong where she had had the most marvelous little silk suits made in only two days.

"And how," Donna thought to herself, "could you ever ask a favor of a terribly glamorous person like that, who has been all over the world and lives in a mansion with all these servants? Why, just listening to her makes me realize what a dowdy little thing I must be."

Still, it was nice to be able to say that her parents would be in India for a month and that they were stopping in Paris on their way home.

"It—it sort of put me on a more equal footing with her," Donna explained to Ricky on Sunday afternoon. "And you know, Rick, by the time we left I wasn't even noticing her weird-colored hair, or that wild costume she was wearing. And although she had sent me out of the room so she could talk to Marjorie, later on she was really awfully nice. Even Jimmy didn't seem to mind too much. At least he stopped grumbling."

Ricky hugged her knees. "Tell me about the house again, Don. And about the dinner. It sounds fabulous, with all those servants and everything."

"Oh!" Donna snapped her fingers. "Did I mention the formal gardens, and the swimming pool? And right back of the swimming pool is this gorgeous, huge greenhouse where the gardener raises millions of flowers—"

She stopped short. Now she was in for it! Why had she ever mentioned the greenhouse?

Sure enough, Ricky had that special light in her eyes. "Flowers? Millions of flowers? Oh, how wonderful, Don!

When will you see her again?"

Donna shook her head. "I don't know, Rick. Maybe never." She took a deep breath. "And I absolutely refuse to ask her to supply the flowers for the spring dance."

Ricky stood up and tightened the belt in her dungarees. "All right, Donna, if that's the way you feel about it, though I must say you aren't showing much school spirit. But would you have any objection to my talking to Miss Dengrove? And if she thinks it's all right, the whole committee could write a letter to Mrs. Cunningham telling her about the dance. Certainly there wouldn't be anything wrong with that."

Donna bit her lip and picked at a broken fingernail. Of course Ricky's suggestion was perfectly proper. Maybe she was wrong to be so timid about asking people for things. The flowers would probably mean nothing to Mrs. Cunningham.

"Why, oh why, didn't I listen to my own better judgment?" she was to say later. "It was all my fault for mentioning the greenhouse that day."

CHAPTER 11   *More Money*

"It sounds perfectly all right to me, if you write the letter," Marjorie Dengrove said after Ricky had discussed the matter with her. "I'm quite sure Mrs. Cunningham will be happy to share some of her flowers with you."

She picked up a pile of papers she had been marking, then stood and stretched. "Oh, what I'd give for a good ice-cream soda now," she yawned. "What a boring Sunday afternoon this is!" She turned to the two girls. "How would you like to drive down to the drug store with me and get a soda? And I have to buy more vitamin pills, too."

"Ooh, we'd love to," said Donna. Ricky nodded.

Miss Dengrove put the marked papers in her briefcase and continued talking. "If only I didn't have that teachers' meeting tomorrow after school; they seem to drag on endlessly. Oh, Donna—" she clapped her forehead. "We simply *must* do some shopping tomorrow, and the bank will be closed before I get out of school. Do you think—" and she paused.

"Tell you what," she went on. "How about taking the check to the drugstore with us? If Doc is on duty, I'm sure he'll cash it. Then I can pick you up here after the meeting tomorrow, and we'll go right to the supermarket."

"Good idea," Donna agreed. "I guess Jimmy won't be home till his usual late hour, so he won't mind. Is he out playing ball now, too?"

"Of course—where else?" The teacher frowned. "You know, something bothers me. I just happened to be teasing Mr. Curtin the other day about how late he keeps the boys at practice, and he looked awfully surprised. He insists they don't stay more than an hour after school. But Jimmy never gets home until dinnertime and vows that he's playing ball all that time."

She slipped into a suede jacket and picked up the car keys. "Poor kid. Mr. Curtin said that the teams will be picked in a week or two, and I guess Jimmy's working extra hard. But I did tell him that he'd have to get home earlier, because it wasn't being very co-operative to keep us waiting. And I told him I had talked to Mr. Curtin, too."

Donna heaved an inward sigh of relief. So Miss Dengrove was keeping an eye on things, after all. Wasn't it lucky that she hadn't written to her parents about Jimmy and gotten them upset, too? Things seemed to have a way of working out.

The ice-cream sodas were delicious, and Doc was gracious about cashing their check.

"Ooh, look!" said Marjorie, picking up a small notebook on the counter. "A budget book! Isn't this cute? It's just what I need, because I'm so awful at keeping track of money."

Donna felt Ricky's elbow nudging her side, but ignored it. As Doc counted out the bills, Marjorie said, "Donna, how about each of us getting a budget book? I'll take care of the food money, and you keep track of the cooky jar money. Here—here's a five-dollar bill and five ones. That'll be enough, won't it?"

Donna nodded. Maybe this would be the solution. This way they could account for every penny. On the other hand, it was the money in the cooky jar that kept disappearing. Why should she be the one to be responsible for that? Could Miss Dengrove really be so clever? Could this all be a plot? Goodness, she was beginning to think like Ricky.

"Could you drop me at my house?" Ricky was saying. "I really must finish my homework."

"And I've got to go back and clean the bird cage, because I never get time during the week." There, Donna thought. Nobody had nagged even once and she had remembered all by herself.

She turned to Ricky. "That man at the zoo must be awfully smart, Rick. The dove's cough is just about gone. Of course, the charcoal was a dreadful mess, but I think I can get rid of it now."

A little while later, having waved good-by to her friend, filled the cooky jar with new bills and placed the budget book beside it, Donna armed herself with a pile of newspapers and prepared to give the cage a thorough cleaning.

"I really must get a new lid for the cooky jar," she thought. "Those crisp green bills are too much of a temptation to anyone coming into the kitchen. Here, birdie, birdie," she cooed.

The dove, now as bright-eyed and active as it had ever been, unexpectedly hopped to her shoulder. Donna stood stock-still, then glided over to the oilcloth-covered table, the bird resting on her shoulder. Stealthily she raised her hands, lifted the bird and set it down on the table.

"We did it! We did it!" she squealed. "I'm sure he's getting used to me now. Oh, wait'll I tell Ricky!"

With a sudden sound, the doorbell rang. Donna jumped. "Can you get it, Donna?" Marjorie called from upstairs.

Donna ran to the front door. Had something happened to Jimmy? Who was this woman standing on the porch? Where had Donna seen her before?

She opened the door cautiously. The woman smiled. "Oh, I'm so glad I found you. You are Donna Parker, aren't you?"

"Why—why, yes, I am. Won't you come in?" She opened the door wider to admit the woman.

"I'm Mrs. Williams. Remember, you baby-sat for me a few months ago?"

"I—I did?"

"Oh, of course, dear. The junior high school sent you over so I could vote in the election, and you took care of Timmy and Ronnie. Remember?"

Donna gaped. Good heavens! How had the woman ever found her? It seemed as though that wild afternoon had happened years ago. Would she ever forget those two little Indians and how exhausted she had been at the end of a few short hours?

She gulped and nodded. "Now I remember, Mrs. Williams. I didn't—"

But she had no chance to finish the sentence.

"I knew you would, dear." The woman rushed on. "Because Timmy and Ronnie have never forgotten *you*. And when a business acquaintance of my husband's called a little while ago and asked us to join him for dinner, why I thought of you immediately. You know, I wouldn't leave my little boys with just anybody."

"I'll bet you wouldn't," Donna thought. "Because practically nobody would stay with them."

"You aren't busy tonight, are you, dear?"

"No," Donna answered, "but I—"

"That's fine, then," Mrs. Williams broke in. "There really will be very little for you to do, dear. I'll have them all fed and ready for bed, and you'll just have to tuck them in and spend a nice quiet evening. We won't be late, and of course Mr. Williams will drive you home. I suppose you charge the regular rates? We'll expect you at seven o'clock, dear. I'm so glad I found you. Remember, three-twenty Locust Street."

She backed out the door, and Donna slowly closed it after her. What had she gotten into? She had hardly opened her mouth, but it seemed that everything was settled.

Oh, well, it couldn't be too bad. At least she wouldn't have to entertain the children, the way she did the last time. And come to think of it, it was a wonderful way to earn money.

"Who was it?" Marjorie called. Donna explained about her new job, and the teacher nodded.

"If you've sat there before, I guess it's all right. I guess we'd better eat dinner a little earlier than usual though, so you'll get there on time."

"Yeeks!" Donna raced down the stairs. "I forgot I was in the midst of cleaning the bird cage."

But where was the dove? Heavens, had she left the door to the back porch open? There sat the bird, on top of the kitchen cupboard that seemed to be its favorite resting place.

"You—you bird, you." Donna shook her finger at the dove. "You know I can't reach all the way up there, even if I stand on a chair. Now get down here immediately!" The bird blinked sleepily.

Donna shrugged her shoulders. "I'll just ignore him," she thought, and went to clean out the cage. As she put the newly scrubbed perch back, she felt something on her shoulder.

"So you came back home, did you?" she murmured. "Now let's have no more nonsense, because I have to go to work tonight."

"I'd better get to the Williamses' a little before seven, so that they can give me instructions," she told Marjorie as they put away the dinner dishes. "Thank goodness Jimmy got home a little earlier today. He does look awfully unhappy, though, doesn't he?"

"Poor kid," Marjorie clucked sympathetically. "I don't understand how a ball game can be so important to anyone. Boys certainly are a problem."

"They certainly are," Donna echoed a little later, as she finished putting Timmy and Ronnie in their beds. Timmy had been surprisingly little trouble; he had only wanted a bedtime story. But two-year-old Ronnie had insisted on surrounding himself with a plush pony, two Teddy bears, a stuffed crocodile, and a huge rabbit with one ear.

"There ought to be a special bed for the toys," Donna thought. "Well, I guess I've got everything now."

She called good night softly and turned off the light.

"Waah!" wailed Ronnie.

The light flicked on.

"Moo bah," he said, pointing vaguely to one corner of the room.

Donna followed his outstretched finger. "What?" she asked.

"Moo bah, moo bah!" he insisted.

"I give up," Donna said aloud, and went into Timmy's darkened room.

"What's a moo bah, Timmy?"

Timmy sat up in his bed. "Oh, Ronnie wants you to turn on his music box when you turn off the light," he explained.

Donna thanked him and tiptoed back. "Here's your music box, Ronnie," she said. "I'll turn it on, and then you can go to sleep." The little boy smiled.

She walked softly down the stairs, listening for sounds from the bedrooms. But all seemed quiet.

As her foot touched the bottom step, there came a loud "Waah!"

She raced up the stairs. "What is it, Ronnie? What happened?"

The sobbing continued, but through it she could make out some peculiar words that sounded very much like

"Mush me choppers, mush me choppers."

"Yeeks!" she sighed, and wearily went back to Timmy's room.

"Timmy," she whispered, "what does 'mush me choppers' mean?"

Timmy giggled. "He means he wants to brush his teeth."

"Now?" Donna asked in amazement. "You mean I have to start all over again?"

It took a full ten minutes for Ronnie to "mush his choppers," get himself surrounded by his toys, and settle himself to go to sleep again.

"The music box," Donna thought instantly, and ran to turn it on before she could hear another "Waah."

And then all was quiet. Really, truly, completely quiet. She finished her homework. She looked at the magazines scattered throughout the living room. She turned on the television set, but could get nothing except some wavy lines. Finally she lay down on the couch.

Then there was the sound of the front door opening, and she jumped up, not knowing at first where she was.

"There you are, dear," Mrs. Williams said. "Was everything fine? I just know it was, and I told everyone tonight what a nice, capable girl you are. It's really such a relief

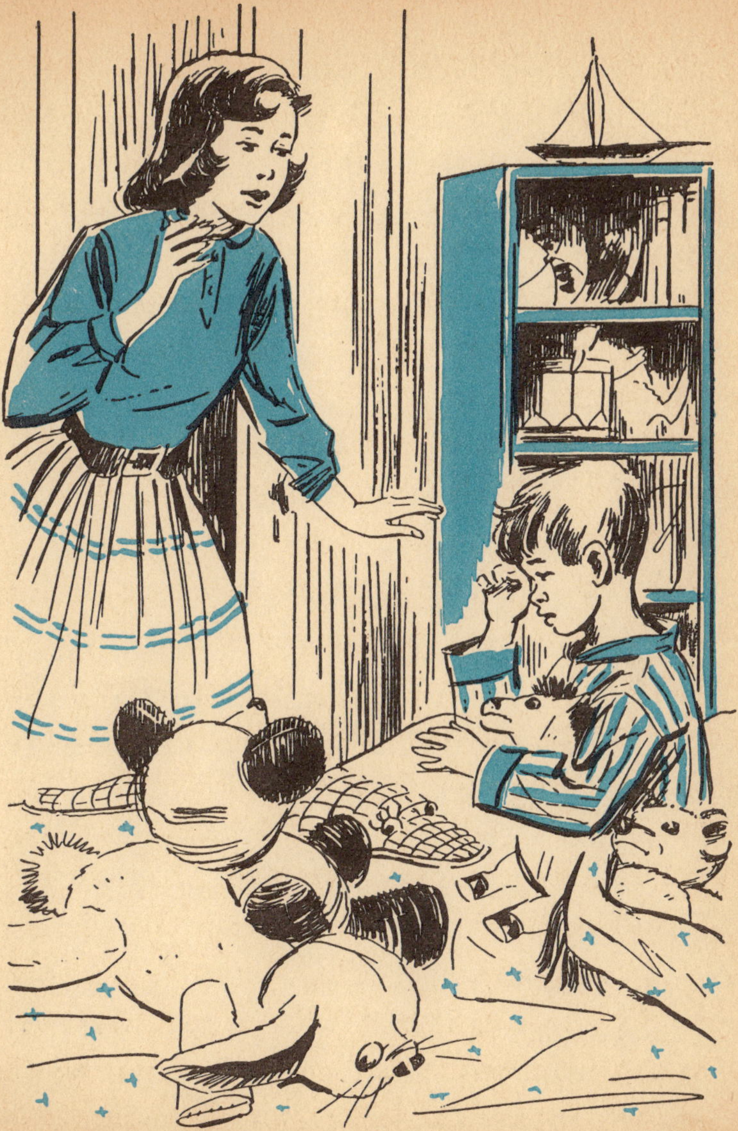

to find someone—well, here's your money, dear, and Mr. Williams is waiting in the car to take you home. Now you just run along—oh, don't forget your coat!"

Donna sleepily wrapped her coat around her, accepted the money Mrs. Williams offered, and did not really awaken until she was upstairs in her own bedroom.

"Wow!" she thought, as she noticed that the hands on her bedside clock pointed to past midnight. "How will I ever get up tomorrow morning?" Then, as she put down the money which she had been holding, "But two and a half dollars in one night! Isn't that wonderful?" And she fell asleep counting piles of dollar bills.

"Don't forget our shopping trip this afternoon, Donna," Marjorie reminded her at breakfast. "Gee, you look tired."

"I am," Donna agreed. "The work wasn't hard last night, but the hours were long. Maybe I'll come home and take a nap until you get here."

"Good idea," Marjorie nodded. "My meeting should be over by four thirty."

But at school, Donna learned that she too had an after-school meeting.

"Not the dance committee again!" she said to Ricky. "Yeeks! I don't see where they find all the things to do."

"Time's growing short," Ricky reminded her. "It's almost Easter, you know. And, Donna, how about the letter to Mrs. Cunningham? Don't you think you should be the one to tell about it, because after all you're the one who met her and who saw the flowers. And Miss Dengrove did say it was all right to ask."

"I guess Ricky's right," Donna thought later. Everyone was tremendously impressed with her account of the greenhouse, and several people came over to congratulate her.

"Gee, Donna, we knew you'd save the day," said Sally Graham. "We can always count on you."

"It really sounds wonderful, Donna," Joyce Davenport said. "I never knew there was a place like that right here in Summerfield. Maybe my father could interview Mrs. Cunningham for the *Daily Bulletin* and run some pictures of her and the house."

Donna was carried along by the enthusiasm of the group, but determined to remain modest. When her name was mentioned to compose the letter to Mrs. Cunningham, she made a short speech.

"I'll write the letter," she said. "But I think all of us should sign it. Or at least it should be signed by George Hart as head of the committee." To herself she said, "At least it won't seem quite so much like a favor to me personally."

"Hear, hear!" everyone cried. "Good old Donna."

"How about doing the letter right now?" Tommy Sheridan suggested as the committee members rose to leave.

Donna looked at the school clock on the wall.

"Yeeks!" she shrieked. "I have to be home at four thirty. I forgot all about shopping with Miss Dengrove. See you later, gang." She picked up her books and fled.

She walked quickly toward the Parker house with a feeling of satisfaction. The tiredness of the early morning had vanished completely. "It's wonderful to be the one everyone looks up to," she thought contentedly. "First, Mother and Daddy going to India. Now, meeting that fabulous Mrs. Cunningham. I guess I'm getting to be sort of a celebrity myself. Gee, everything's getting to be so much fun."

The Parker car was standing at the curb, and Donna rushed into the house.

"Marjorie, Margie," she panted. "Am I late?"

"Just got in myself," the teacher replied. "Here's a letter from your folks."

"Goody." She grabbed the letter and tore it open. "They're in Madras," she explained a few seconds later. "And the temperature is over ninety. Imagine! Mommy says it's so exciting and romantic—coconut trees, and bullock wagons in the streets, and a little thatched-roof village right next to their air-conditioned hotel. And, oh, listen, Margie."

She turned the page. "Mommy says why don't I have a party, if it's all right with you?"

She hugged herself. "Oh, wouldn't that be scrumptious, Marjorie? Do you think I could?"

Marjorie nodded, and Donna gave her a tight squeeze. Then she became thoughtful. "I have the two and a half dollars that I earned last night, and maybe I can earn some more. I'll keep track of it all in my little budget book."

Letter still in hand, she went out to the kitchen. "I guess it belongs here, under miscellaneous," she murmured. "Let's see, that's two-fifty for baby-sitting, and ten dollars I put in the cooky jar yesterday—" Absent-mindedly she fingered the bills in the jar.

Then she straightened up and laid down the pencil she had been holding.

Where was the five-dollar bill? The five ones were all

there, but the five-dollar bill was definitely gone. This time there was no mistaking it.

White-faced, she walked back into the living room and stood before the teacher.

"Marjorie," she said, and her voice shook, "Marjorie, the five-dollar bill I put in the cooky jar is missing now. Do you know anything about it?"

CHAPTER 12 *The Dean's Office*

The teacher opened her mouth to speak.

And at that moment the doorbell rang. Donna twirled around. Why did this have to happen now?

Miss Dengrove went to open the door, leaving Donna clenching her fists. What had Marjorie been about to say?

"Why, Mr. Curtin, what are you doing here? And Jimmy, too. Is anything wrong?" The teacher looked from the man to Donna's brother.

The baseball coach gave Jimmy a gentle shove into the house and stepped inside himself.

"Not a thing, Miss Dengrove," said the man with a twinkle in his blue eyes. "I just wanted to prove to you that practice really is over at a reasonable hour, as I said. And I decided that the best way to make my point was to deliver Jimmy to his doorstep."

Jimmy started to protest. "But I only—"

"Never mind, young man." The coach patted him on the shoulder. "I'm sure Miss Dengrove has enough troubles without worrying about whether you'll be home for dinner on time. By the way"—and he turned to the teacher again and grinned—"how *are* you getting along? Tell me how a little scatterbrain like you can take care of a house and two children. I know you're a great first-grade teacher, but as a housekeeper—"

"Shush," said Miss Dengrove, but she dimpled as though she knew that Mr. Curtin didn't mean a word that he had said. "You mustn't talk about me like that in front of my two charges. Do you want to undermine all their respect for me?"

Then she went over to Donna and put her arm around the girl's waist. "We're getting along just fine, aren't we, honey?"

Donna nodded. What could she say?

Marjorie tilted her head and looked up at the coach. "Just because I always run short of money before payday doesn't mean I'm completely irresponsible, you know. It's all because this silly school system pays its teachers once a month, and it's such a terribly long time between checks."

Mr. Curtin grinned, as though he had heard Marjorie's complaint many times and knew what was coming next.

"Go on," he said. "Now tell me that part about how a girl like you is used to getting her allowance each week, and it's not fair to make you plan every penny a whole month ahead."

Then he became serious. "Good heavens, Miss Dengrove, don't you realize that a great many teachers support whole families on what you're earning? Of course, they don't buy alligator handbags and cashmere sweaters."

Donna had never seen Marjorie pouting, but she certainly was doing that now. Then the young woman raised her head and with a determined air said, "Well, we're doing fine now. Donna and I each have our own budget books. We're going to keep track of every penny, aren't we, Donna?"

Again Donna nodded, glumly. In a weak voice she started to say, "That five dollars that was in the cooky jar—"

But Marjorie was pointing to her purse and saying, "I've got twenty dollars here right now. We're going shopping at the supermarket, and I shall write down all the money we spend. I even thought ahead yesterday and we cashed Mrs. Parker's check at the drugstore."

Mr. Curtin shook his head sadly. "I can see I'll really have to take you in hand. You could have saved yourself a trip. Didn't you know that the supermarket will be glad to cash your check for you, if you show them some kind of identification?"

He picked up his hat, which he had placed on the hall table, and said, "Come on, girls. I'd better go shopping with you, or you'll end up with all sorts of fancy crackers and *pâté de foie gras* and caviar, and nothing to make a meal of."

"Why you—you—" Marjorie stammered. Then she smiled. "Why, thank you, sir," she said demurely. "You may carry all the packages for us." And taking Donna by the arm, she led her down the front steps.

"Come on, Jimmy," called Mr. Curtin. Reluctantly the boy slouched out the door, slamming it after him. "Shopping with the women," he mumbled. "Just like I was a baby and had to tag along."

"Wait till Mr. Curtin sees what a wonderful teen-age party we give you, Donna," Marjorie said in a loud whisper as they parked the car in the supermarket lot. "Then he won't think I'm such a scatterbrain. We'll make it a real super-duper one."

Donna looked at the young woman, her eyes shining. "Oh, could we really, Marjorie? I'd be scared to do it by myself. Mother always plans my parties for me and makes all the refreshments. I just help, and that's no fun."

But she had always wanted to give a party by herself, Donna thought. This would be one party that would be run the way she wanted it. But what kind should it be?

"We could have do-it-yourself sundaes," Marjorie was saying, "and maybe that wonderful sandwich loaf I make with the cream cheese frosting...." She paused and looked up at Mr. Curtin, who was taking a shopping cart from the series of wire baskets lined up near the door.

"Of course, we've got to keep the cost down. But that won't be too difficult."

The cost! Donna put her hand to her mouth. How could she ever afford to give a party? Especially if money kept disappearing. She had better take the rest of the bills out of the cooky jar. No, she would leave a dollar bill there, just to see what happened.

Maybe Miss Dengrove really was scatterbrained, as Mr. Curtin had said. Maybe she had helped herself to the money and forgotten to tell Donna. Maybe she had been raised differently, and didn't think certain things were important.

But it wasn't fair of the coach to be so hard on her—after all, she had never run a house before, and she was obviously used to having loads of money to spend.

And it was awfully sweet of her to offer to help with the party. Wouldn't it be terrif if they gave a really unusual kind, one that the gang would talk about for weeks afterwards?

She squeezed Miss Dengrove's hand. "I'm so glad you're here," she said. What was a mere five-dollar bill? She would make the money somehow.

As Miss Dengrove unlocked the door to the Parker house, the telephone rang.

"I'll get it," Donna said, putting her bag of groceries on the hall table. Mr. Curtin and Jimmy trooped into the kitchen behind her, laden with boxes, carriers of coke, and bags of potatoes and oranges.

"I hope it's Mrs. Williams," she thought. "It would be nice to get paid again for doing my homework—and taking care of the boys, of course."

But it was not Mrs. Williams. It was Mrs. Mitchell, a friend of the Parkers, with an invitation for dinner for the next night.

"I should have asked you before I accepted," Donna said

to Marjorie. "But I thought you'd like to go. Her husband is an architect and they just built this gorgeous, very modern house that I've been dying to see. Mommy and Daddy were invited there just before they left for India, and they said it's absolutely sensational. Wasn't it nice of her to ask us? And you too, Jimmy."

"Now, Jimmy," Mr. Curtin said, rumpling the boy's hair. "Remember you're the man of the house. And don't forget, we choose teams next week. You've got a lot of hard practicing ahead of you."

Marjorie walked with Mr. Curtin to the door to thank him for his help.

"Phone's ringing," she called to Donna, who was still in the kitchen.

Donna lifted the receiver. "Yes, Mrs. Williams, I'd love to, but—" She waited for the woman to stop talking long enough for her to get a word in. "But you see, we're going out to dinner tomorrow night. Eight thirty? Yes, I guess we'll be through by then. Well, yes, I guess Miss Dengrove could drop me off on my way home. Thank you."

"Wow!" She wiped her forehead. "That woman doesn't take No for an answer. Oh, well, I did want to earn more money for my party."

The next evening at the Mitchells', however, she vowed she would never again accept two dates for one evening.

First, there had been the problem with Jimmy. She and Marjorie had waited and waited, and finally at five thirty had left a note for him, telling him to come to the Mitchells' on his bicycle.

"And if he misses dinner, it'll just be his own fault," his sister had said, tacking the note to the front door. "After all Mr. Curtin said about coming right home, too."

But she need not have feared. Even after a tour of the glass and brick house, of the strange cubicles of bedrooms and the skylighted kitchen; even after Mrs. Mitchell had served fruit juice and crackers in the dramatic living room with its sunken circular fireplace and three walls made entirely of glass; even after Jimmy had finally bicycled up, grimy and uncombed, and been sent to wash; even then dinner was not served.

For, as they were enjoying the view of the sunset and sipping their juice, just as Donna was thinking how wonderful it must be to live in such an elegant house with all the latest conveniences, three men appeared outside the glass door.

"Photographers," Mrs. Mitchell said, as her husband

unfolded himself from a low canvas chair and went to greet them.

Donna and Marjorie raised their eyebrows questioningly.

"To take pictures of the house," their hostess explained. "This is supposed to be one of the foremost examples of modern architecture in the country, and it's always being written up in magazines. It's quite an honor, you know. I never know when people are coming in to take pictures and do articles, so I have to be ready at all times." She quickly cleared away the tray of crackers and the glasses, though Donna had not finished her juice.

"These men are from *Modern Home,*" she continued, fluffing up pillows and moving her guests to one side of the room, "and they want to show that a house as well-designed as this one is not only beautiful to look at, but also comfortable to live in."

"It is?" thought Donna, looking around her with a new eye.

"But how can you work in a kitchen without a single window to look out of?" she thought, as the photographers posed Mrs. Mitchell mixing a salad.

"And how do you get any privacy?" she wondered, as she noticed that the bedroom walls reached only three-quarters of the way to the ceiling, and noise floated from one end of the house to the other. But the photographers were using words like "functional" and "organic," and seemed delighted.

"Imagine not having to dust books," whispered Marjorie, as Mr. Mitchell opened the doors of several cabinets in the living room and revealed shelves of reading material.

"But I like to look at books," Donna thought stubbornly. "And I think rows of bright covers are much warmer looking than plain white cupboard doors, even if you do have to dust them. Isn't it funny? I oohed and aahed when I came here—I guess everybody does—but for comfortable living, I'll take our little old house. This looks so wonderful, but I'd feel that I was living in a goldfish bowl."

"I'm hungry," Jimmy grumbled, no longer interested in all the angled shots the photographers were taking.

"And I'm going to be late to the Williamses'," Donna thought in panic. "If Mother had been home, she never would have let me go baby-sitting tonight."

Long after dark the men packed up their cameras and tripods, and dinner was finally served.

"Yeeks!" Donna said as she looked out of the side window of the car a little later. "Wasn't that a wild evening?

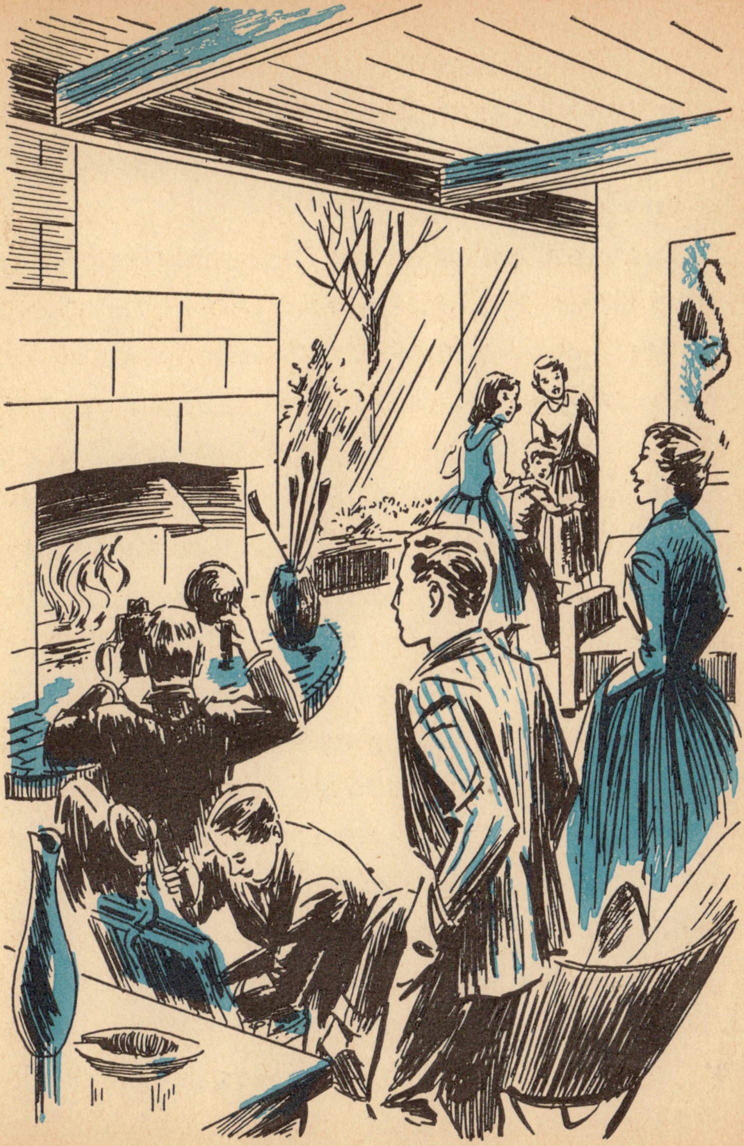

Imagine not being able to put a newspaper down because someone might want to take a picture of the room. I guess it's no fun living in a showplace, even if it does have a lot of bathrooms and a dishwasher."

In fact, she would have much preferred going back to her own house and appreciating the luxury of being able to sit wherever she wanted, or to leave her books on the hall table, rather than going to the Williamses'.

"I really can't complain, though," she thought, as she settled herself to her homework. "One good thing about baby-sitting so late is that I didn't even have to put the boys to bed. Mrs. Williams is a little dizzy, and she talks a blue streak, but she's really quite nice."

"And somehow," she thought as she finished the last of her assignments, "I seem to get more work done here. I'll have a chance now to write to Mommy and Daddy, and to prepare that letter to Mrs. Cunningham about the flowers, before Mr. and Mrs. Williams get back."

Well-pleased with herself, she thought over the events of the last few days.

"Mommy will be so surprised at how grown-up I've become," she thought. "I'm glad she's enjoying India, but in a way this is a vacation for me, too. It's fun getting out and meeting people like Mrs. Cunningham and the Mitchells, and not being known as Grace Parker's daughter, but a person in my own right. It's fun to plan a party with Marjorie, although I will say it was nice of Mommy to suggest it. And it's fun to earn money that's all my own, and not have Mommy saying 'Donna, you need your sleep. Donna, you must be in bed by ten o'clock.'"

She chewed on her pencil. "I'll bet even Jimmy enjoys the change, though you can't really tell with him. I wonder why he was so late getting to the Mitchells'. I didn't even get a chance to ask him."

Her mind wandered on. "And I wonder if that dollar that I left in the cooky jar will still be there when I get home." Her head began to nod. "Could I possibly be all wrong about Marjorie? Could the money be vanishing some other way? She never did answer my question. I wonder what Mommy . . . ."

Her head snapped up. Goodness, Mrs. Williams should have been home by now. She was getting awfully sleepy.

But all that lovely money that Mrs. Williams gave her a long half hour later made her forget her tiredness, and she agreed to come again the following evening.

"My," Mrs. Williams laughed. "You're going to have

to move in here as a full-time boarder, Donna. But really, dear, I was saying to May Mackay only tonight, you don't know what a relief it is—well, you'd better run. School tomorrow, you know!" she finished brightly.

"If only I hadn't promised," Donna thought as she walked home from school the next afternoon. Another meeting of the dance committee and some extra work for the newspaper had prevented her from getting home in time to take the nap she longed for.

"I guess Mommy's right about that ten o'clock bedtime after all. I don't know how Marjorie does it, staying up so late night after night."

She plopped herself down on her bed. "That math test today!" She shuddered. "I really knew it last night, but my head ached so today that every bit I had learned disappeared. Why, I almost fell asleep in the middle of it. And science tomorrow! I hope I get a chance to rest at the Williamses'."

But the evening worked out far differently from what Donna had hoped. Ronnie seemed to be having bad dreams, and his cries and troubled sleep kept Donna running up and down the stairs.

And Timmy explained that he had taken a long nap that

afternoon, and now could he see television or play with his new fire engine, because he wasn't sleepy at all.

Donna tried bedtime stories, and lullabies, and a stern attitude, and pleading, all to no avail. Timmy finally dropped off to sleep a few minutes before Mr. and Mrs. Williams returned.

By that time Donna's headache was worse, and though she slept soundly at home, morning came all too soon.

The science test, as she had feared, was torture. Her head throbbed, and the words danced before her eyes. Several times she felt the teacher looking at her strangely.

A yellow slip which was delivered to her toward the end of the day, saying she was to report to the dean of girls after school, made her heart pound as hard as her head.

She knocked timidly at the door marked MRS. THOMAS.

"Well, now, Donna," said the gray-haired woman sitting behind the desk, "what's troubling you? How are you getting along without your mother? Do you miss her very much?"

Donna looked at the dean in surprise. Miss her mother? She shook her head, then nodded it. "Oh, of course I miss her, and Daddy, too. But nothing's wrong. We're getting along just fine with Miss Dengrove."

"I'm glad to hear that, Donna. Several teachers have told me that you haven't been looking well. And your work hasn't been up to your usual standards."

Mrs. Thomas glanced at some papers on her desk. "You flunked a math test earlier this week, and a science test today. That's not like you."

"I—I did?" Donna bit her lower lip. She squirmed in her chair. "It's just—just—well," she blurted out, "I haven't been getting enough sleep because I've been baby-sitting to make some money so I could have a party." She looked down at her lap.

Mrs. Thomas leaned back. "So that's it. Well, my dear, no more baby-sitting for you for quite a while." The woman's tone was kind but firm.

Donna sighed. Sometimes it was nice to have somebody tell you that you couldn't do something. Mrs. Thomas was a very motherly kind of person.

"I guess you're right," Donna admitted.

"And is that the only thing that's been bothering you, Donna? Come on, speak up."

Donna stared at her shoes. There was still that business about the money. It seemed that every time she started to discuss it with Marjorie, something happened.

And as she got to know the teacher better, it became harder and harder to believe that she had anything to do with the disappearing bills. But what else could have happened to them?

"No, there's really nothing wrong." Donna smiled weakly and rose to leave. Her head was still throbbing.

"Remember now, plenty of sleep for you, Miss Donna." Mrs. Thomas walked with her to the door. "Young people sometimes don't know their own limits."

And that was a remark Donna was to think of many times in the next week.

CHAPTER 13   *The Party*

"Do you really think we can do all this by next Friday?" Donna said to Marjorie, looking at the papers which almost covered the kitchen table. Each one contained a list for the party.

Marjorie continued writing. "And for the sandwich loaf we'll need tuna fish, and eggs for egg salad, and loads of cream cheese. Did you say eight boys and eight girls, Donna?"

"She didn't even hear me," Donna thought in distress. "How are we ever going to decorate the living room, and do all the shopping, and make all these fancy refreshments by next Saturday night?"

It had been Marjorie's idea to have a square-dance party, and everyone at school had thought it was wonderful.

"Everyone but me," Donna sighed. "I never realized that

there were so many things to worry about, like what kind of paper plates to buy, and how many bottles of soda pop you need for sixteen people."

She thought back to her conversation with Mrs. Thomas. A few nights' sleep had made all the difference, of course. But here she was, involved in a party that was turning out to be a lot more work than she had bargained for. She just hoped that Marjorie knew what she was doing.

The teacher looked up. "Come on, honey. Smile! You look so worried all the time, like a little old lady. You'll get wrinkles in your face that way," she teased. "I promise I won't let you down. Now you promise to look more cheerful."

"I promise." Donna smiled. Marjorie was right. The party was sure to be a success. The girls were already talking about the bright-colored skirts they were going to wear, and the boys had agreed to come in dungarees and gay shirts.

"I used to be the caller for square dances when I went to college," Marjorie said, "and I still have some wonderful records. And Mr. Curtin said he would lend us his record player."

Ricky kept telephoning to learn more about the party,

but Donna had agreed with Marjorie that the details should be kept secret.

"Like the sundaes," the teacher said enthusiastically. "We'll have everything out on the table—ice cream and chocolate sauce and mashmallow whip and cherries and bananas and nuts. Then we'll give one prize to the person who makes the prettiest sundae, and one to the person who makes the most original sundae."

Donna hugged her knees. "The boys will love that," she said. "And that was a wonderful idea about the broom dance. And the balloon dance is great, where everyone tries to puncture the balloons tied around the girls' ankles, and the last couple with a balloon wins. Oh, I'm sure it will be a super party, Margie."

Still, there was all that work to be done, and Jimmy refused to lift a hand to help. "It's your party, not mine," he said. "And I gotta get in all the practice I can, because Friday Mr. Curtin is going to tell us who made the team."

"I'm glad we were able to do almost all the shopping last Saturday," Donna said the afternoon of the party.

"And I got home from school very early today," said Marjorie. "See!" She opened the refrigerator door. "The egg salad and the tuna fish salad are already made."

Donna clapped her hands. "Oh, Margie, you're wonderful." Why had she ever doubted her?

"Now while you roll up the rug in the living room," the teacher said, "and set out the paper plates and things, I'll run down to the store and get the ice cream and the bread for the sandwich loaf."

"I can't wait," said Donna. "Does the cream-cheese frosting really make it look like a cake, Margie?"

Miss Dengrove nodded. "Honest and truly," she said, reaching for her handbag. "I'll only be a few minutes," she called from the front hall.

Donna quickly set out the plates, and straws for the coke bottles, and small dishes in which the sundaes were to be made.

She struggled with the rug, which refused to roll up evenly. "If only someone were here to lift the chairs while I get this old rug out from under," she thought, gritting her teeth.

Where was Marjorie? She should have been back from the store by now. At first Donna was annoyed that the teacher had not returned more quickly. Then as it grew dark, and she still had not returned from her errand, Donna became concerned.

"I hope she wasn't in an accident," she thought, standing at the living-room window. She had done everything she could think of for tonight. The living room looked festive, with balloons clustered on the walls and red and white crepe paper stretching from opposite ends of the ceiling. Just the sandwich loaf remained to be made. But what could have happened to Marjorie?

She heard a door close. Was the teacher coming in the back way?

"Oh, it's just you," she said as her brother appeared in the kitchen. "I can't imagine what's happened to Marjorie, Jimmy. Did you see her?"

Jimmy shrugged. "Her? She can stay away forever, for all I care. I hate her—her and that dopey coach."

"Jimmy! You mustn't talk like that! Miss Dengrove is a very nice person. And," turning back to the living room, "I wish I knew what has happened to her. Oh, dear, oh, dear. She's been gone for practically hours." She paced up and down the room.

The sound of a car in the driveway made her fling open the door.

"Margie, Margie, is that you?" she called.

A breathless figure ran up the steps to the porch.

"Were you worried, Donna?" the teacher asked, putting several packages on the kitchen table. "You'll never know the trouble I had."

"The car?" Donna asked.

Miss Dengrove shook her head. "No, just getting plain unsliced bread for the sandwich loaf. I drove all over town and there wasn't one single loaf of white bread that wasn't sliced. They didn't even understand what I was talking about when I said I wanted to slice it the long way, like a layer cake, instead of up and down."

"But did you—"

"I did! Somebody finally suggested Deutsch's Bakery, way at the other end of town. They had just finished the afternoon baking and the man grabbed a loaf before it went through the slicing machine."

"Thank goodness!" Donna sighed in relief. "We'll really have to rush, now."

"Hey!" Jimmy had been standing near the refrigerator. "When do I get supper?"

Donna and Marjorie exchanged glances. Why, they had been so busy preparing for the party that they had completely forgotten about their own dinner.

"Come on, Jimmy," said Marjorie. "I'll make you some

tuna fish and egg salad sandwiches from the party food."

"No, thank *you*," Jimmy said emphatically. Miss Dengrove went over to him, but he squirmed away and ran upstairs.

"Oh, he'll get over it," said Donna. "I've never known Jimmy to go without a meal yet. I'll just leave some things in the refrigerator for him. We can eat while we're working."

"You run upstairs and get dressed," Marjorie said a little while later. "I'll finish up this little bit. Don't things look pretty?" She stepped back to admire her handiwork.

"Beautiful," Donna agreed, her eyes shining. "Oh, Margie, you're a doll!"

What was it that Mrs. Thomas had said, Donna thought, as she put on her red skirt with the little black hearts scattered on it—that thing about young people not knowing their own limits? It had worried her all week. In fact, it had taken away most of the joy in giving the party. This was so much more ambitious than the usual hamburger-and-coke-and-social-dancing parties that everyone gave.

She tied a red ribbon in her dark hair, fluffed out her skirts, and hugged her old stuffed animal for good luck.

"It's going to be a wonderful evening, Puppy, I just know it." And she flew down the steps.

"Here they come!" she called, as she heard the tramping of feet on the front steps. "Ooh, I'm so nervous!"

"Say, this looks real fancy," said little Tommy Sheridan, as he gazed at the festive-looking living room.

"We're all ready to learn them square dances," called Jack Kingston with a cowboy twang.

"Hey, Bill, that's a real smooth shirt you're wearing," said Steve Collins. "What color is it?" For Bill Blanchard's flannel shirt was an unmistakable, brilliant, eye-shattering red.

"Everything looks super," Ricky whispered. "And you look awfully cute, Donna. I'll put the coats up in your bedroom. All right?"

Donna nodded, her cheeks flaming with excitement.

Just then Marjorie appeared. "In a few minutes, after they get settled, tell the boys to choose partners," she said to Donna. "Four sets of partners to a group, and each group forms a little circle."

When Ricky came downstairs, Donna clapped her hands and repeated the instructions the teacher had given her.

At first there was complete bedlam, but finally things

settled down. Everyone listened to Marjorie as she explained how to sashay, how to allemande, and how to swing your partner.

"We did this at camp last summer when we went to visit the boys at Three Pines," thought Donna as they circled around. "Gee, I had forgotten all about that."

She caught Ricky's eye and the red-haired girl nodded, seeming to catch Donna's thought. "I remember too," her eager smile said.

The music was lively, the boys and girls learned quickly, and Marjorie seemed to know an endless number of dances.

"Wow, I'm beat," said George Hart, sinking to the floor in a mock faint at the end of a wild Virginia Reel.

"Me, too," everyone murmured, finding places to sit on chairs, sofas, and floor.

"Should we serve now?" Marjorie asked Donna in a low voice.

Donna agreed and clapped her hands for quiet.

"What we all need is something to give us a little energy. How about—food?"

There was a loud cheer and everyone started for the dining room. Marjorie had ducked into the kitchen, and now on the dining room table sat two frosted "cakes."

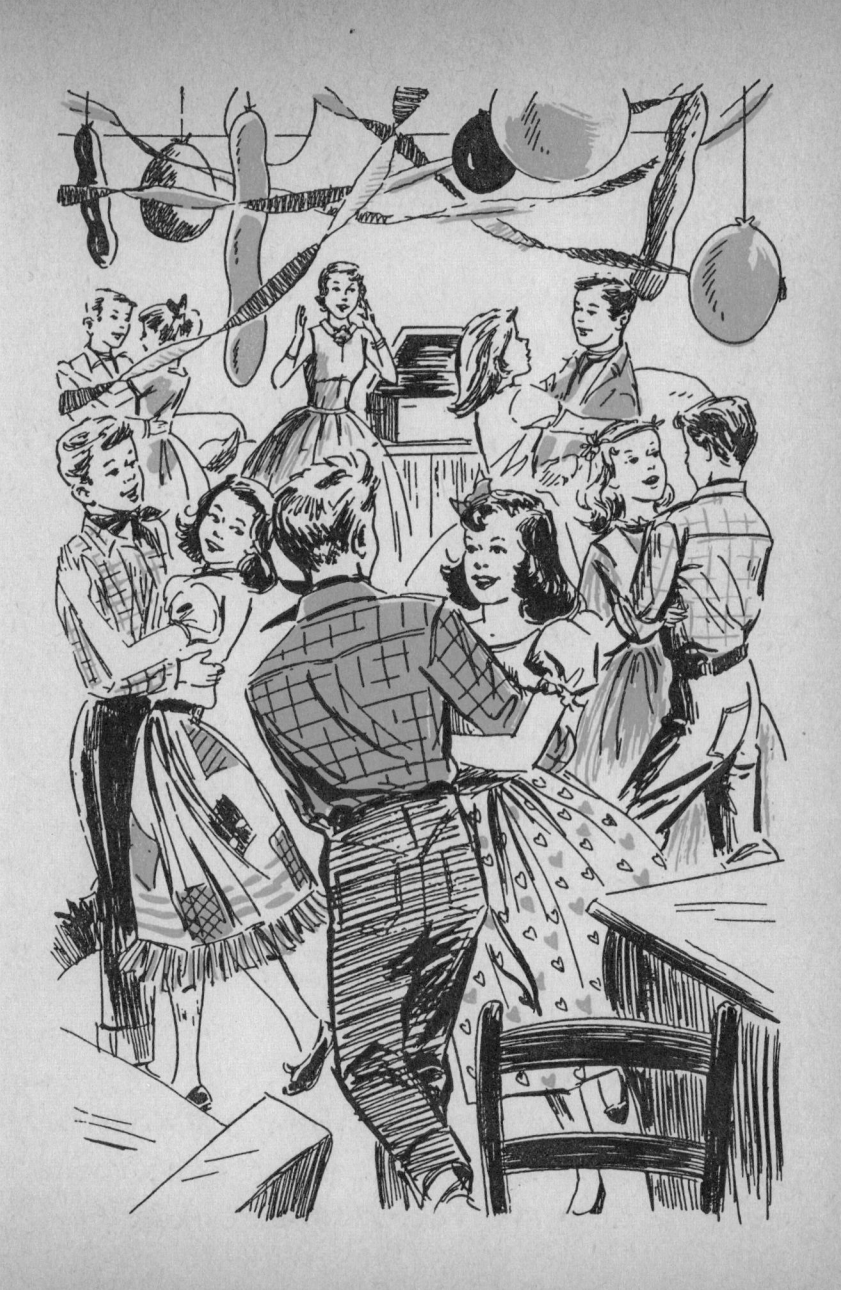

"A nickel to anyone who guesses what kind of filling the cake has," Donna called above the voices as she picked up a knife to cut slices.

There was a murmur of astonishment as they watched and then tasted.

"It's so queer to expect something sweet, and instead taste—tuna fish!" Tommy Sheridan said. "But it's awfully good, Donna."

And from the way the sandwiches and the soda pop disappeared, Donna could tell everyone was happy.

"And now, for dessert, we have a contest," she announced. She explained the rules for do-it-yourself sundaes.

"Just what we've always dreamed about," said several of the boys. "Oh, baby, all the whipped cream we want."

"I guess I should have added that they have to eat whatever they make," Donna thought in dismay. Even the girls were loading their plates with dozens of cherries and spoonful after spoonful of chocolate sauce.

"Wow, I'm dripping all over the place," called Jack Kingston, as he noticed a train of chocolate syrup all the way into the living room.

"Oh, we'll wipe it up later," Donna called. She knew her

mother would have gotten a cloth immediately, and everyone would have helped her clean up the bits of nuts on the floor, and the melted ice cream, and the soda that had spilled. And then everyone would have quieted down and tried not to cause any more bother—and been subdued and uncomfortable.

"But it will be just as easy to clean up later, won't it, and not spoil the whole party?" she thought.

Joyce Davenport's dessert, looking so professional with its neat swirl of whipped cream topped by a cherry, won the prize for the prettiest sundae. And little blue-eyed Karen won the prize for the most original, with a jolly face made of vanilla ice cream with banana slices for eyes, cherries for teeth, and chopped nuts for hair.

"Ooh, it was the most marvelous, scrumptious, magnificent party I've ever had," Donna said after the last guest had gone. "Did you hear all the nice things the whole gang said when they left? I'll bet they'll be telling about it for weeks."

She grabbed Marjorie by the waist and danced her around the living room. "And it's all because of you. Oh, how can I ever thank you enough!"

"I'm sort of tuckered out, kiddo," the teacher flopped into

the nearest chair. "What say we just leave everything as is, and clean up in the morning? Oh, I forgot to tell you, Donna. Gladell called before you got home from school this afternoon and asked if she could come to clean tomorrow instead of Tuesday."

"Yeeks!" thought Donna. "Wait'll she sees this mess! She'll have fits. I'm as tired as Marjorie though. If I go to bed now, I'll be able to get up first thing in the morning and straighten up before Gladell gets here."

"I guess we really ought to put the food away," Miss Dengrove was saying. "Not that there's much food left, unless you count the crumbs all over this floor. Sa-ay"—she straightened up in the chair—"I wonder whether Jimmy ever got anything to eat."

"I'll run up and see whether he's asleep," Donna offered. "Though how he could sleep with all that noise, I don't know."

She was down in a few seconds.

"Margie, he isn't in his room. And his bed hasn't been touched. You know, I didn't see him all evening."

"Neither did I." Marjorie stood up. "But he must be someplace around. Maybe he was mad about our not getting him any dinner, and he wants to scare us. Well, he's got to be someplace."

But Jimmy was nowhere upstairs. He was nowhere downstairs.

"How about the cellar?" Marjorie asked. "Sometimes he likes to play ball down there."

Donna shook her head. "No. I looked. Oh, Marjorie, what could have happened to him? It's after eleven o'clock! I—I don't even know where to begin to look!"

CHAPTER 14 — *Jimmy*

"Well, he's got to be someplace," said the teacher, obviously trying to cheer Donna. "Now let's think where he could be."

There was a moment's silence. Donna leaned her head against the wall. If she could only *think*. "Did he say he was going to visit anyone, Margie?"

Miss Dengrove snapped her fingers. "That's an idea. He didn't say, but could he have gone to someone's house to sleep?"

"We could try Skipper Gray, next door. It's awfully late to call, but if he isn't there maybe Skipper could tell us where to find him. Those two kids get all sorts of crazy ideas."

Donna dialed the number, and a sleepy voice answered the phone.

"I'm terribly sorry to bother you so late at night, Mrs. Gray," Donna began. "But we just wondered if Jimmy happened to be staying overnight at your house."

She shook her head sadly in answer to Marjorie's unspoken question. "Well, do you have any idea where he might be? No, he came home after school. Yes, we looked all over the house. I was having a party tonight and we didn't notice that he wasn't in his room until a few minutes ago."

She paused a moment. "That's a good idea, Mrs. Gray. Thanks ever so much. Oh, I'm sure we'll find him."

She turned to the teacher. "She suggested trying the Recreation Center and the movies. It's very late for him to be at either place, but he may have gone just to get out of the house."

Miss Dengrove picked up her coat. "I'll drive over, Donna. Do you want to come with me, or do you want to stay here?"

"I don't know." The girl shivered slightly. "I suppose I ought to stay here, in case he comes back but—could we leave him a note, and tell him we'll be right back?"

"Of course, honey," said Miss Dengrove. "We'll only be a few minutes, anyhow."

But they were longer than Marjorie had expected. The Recreation Center was just closing and the janitor assured Donna that no small boys had been there all evening.

"Friday is Business Men's Night," he said, turning off lights in the gym. "No kids here tonight. Only men."

The cashier at the movies tried to be helpful and allowed Donna to go into the darkened theater.

"He certainly isn't there," Donna said when she came back to the parked car. "There aren't more than a dozen people inside, and the usher said all the children had left hours ago. Oh, Margie, what do we do now?"

"First, let's go home." The teacher made a U-turn in the deserted street. "He may have come back by now." She looked at Donna for a second, then back at the street. "I'm sure he's perfectly all right, honey. Now don't go worrying again. Remember how much fun we had this evening?"

"It seems years," said Donna. Less than an hour ago she had been so happy. The party had been more successful than she had dreamed possible.

"They're all such nice boys and girls, too," Marjorie was saying, trying to keep Donna's mind occupied. "Who's that tall blond girl?"

"You must mean Anne Franklin," Donna said. "She's

an awfully sweet person, isn't she?"

"She was telling me about her pets," the teacher said. "She must love animals."

"Oh, I meant to show her my dove," Donna reminded herself.

"Didn't she tell you? Well, I guess there was too much going on." The teacher stopped to wait for a red light to change. "While the others were eating, she came back into the kitchen with me and asked to see your bird."

"I'm glad," Donna said. "Did she like it?"

"Very much." The light turned green. "She even took it out of its cage and let it fly around the kitchen for a few minutes. And do you know, I think that bird must have known what she was saying."

"Really?" Donna turned around to face the teacher. "What did it do?"

"Oh, it hopped around on the counters, and flew to her shoulder and then to her hand. It was really exciting to watch."

"Isn't that wonderful!" Donna said. "I really must spend some time with the bird so I can surprise Daddy when he gets back. Oh!"

They had arrived at the Parker house. "I almost forgot

about Jimmy," she said, opening the car door. "He simply must be home by now."

But the note was just where they left it. And Jimmy was still nowhere in sight.

"Should we—do you think we ought to—call the police?" Donna asked in a small voice. If anything had happened to Jimmy, it would be her fault! How would she ever face her parents again? How would she ever be able to live with herself?

"I guess we should," Marjorie agreed, now looking almost as upset as Donna. "I simply don't understand what has happened to him."

She walked toward the telephone in the kitchen, then paused at the door to the cellar stairs.

"Come here, Donna," she whispered.

Donna leaned her head toward the darkened cellar. "It —it sounds like a sort of scratching, or sniffing, or something. Is it a mouse, do you think?"

Marjorie smiled slightly. "No, I don't think so." She switched on the cellar lights.

"But I looked there," Donna protested, following Marjorie down the stairs.

The teacher wended her way past old chairs, castoff

wagons and bicycles, and pieces of lumber.

"There are only piles of screens over there," Donna said. Marjorie put a finger to her lips.

"Not just screens," she said, as she stooped down and looked into the triangle of space made by the screens leaning sharply against the cellar wall.

"Go 'way," said a small boy's voice.

Donna gasped. "Jimmy, Jimmy!"

She peeped into the triangle, then sent the screens crashing on the cellar floor. There sat her little brother, huddled against the wall, his face tearstained and streaked with dirt.

Donna pulled him out, and he came reluctantly. She hugged him close. Surprisingly, he did not pull away.

"Jimmy, Jimmy! You had us scared almost to death. Didn't you hear us calling and calling? We looked for you all over town, and we were just ready to call the police."

Jimmy's sniffs grew louder.

"You poor kid," Marjorie said. "Sitting here all alone in the dark. And I'll bet you haven't had anything to eat. I'll go right upstairs and fix you some nice hot chocolate."

But after the teacher left, the boy still hung back.

"What's the matter, Jimmy?" Donna asked. "Was the party too noisy? Is that why you came down here?"

Her brother shook his head. "Then what's the trouble?" She looked at his sad little face. "Did something happen at school?"

"Nobody even cares about me," he sniffed. "You and that—that teacher were so busy with your old party you never even asked me about . . . about . . . ." He sniffed again.

Donna's mouth opened. "Oh, Jimmy, your team! Today was the day the team was picked, and we didn't even ask you about it. Did you get on it, Jimmy?"

He shook his head and looked at the floor. "No—no, I didn't." Then he looked up at his sister and his eyes flashed. "And I know why, too. It isn't fair!"

"What isn't fair, Jimmy?"

"Just—just because old Dengrove told Mr. Curtin I wasn't co-operating, like he told me to . . . ." His voice faded off, and he began again. "Just because I wasn't home in time to go to the silly old Mitchell house, when I don't even know them and anyhow, I had to practice that pitch . . . ." Again his voice faltered.

"Jimmy!" Donna looked at him in amazement. "Do you really believe that Marjorie told Mr. Curtin not to put you on the team? Is that why you're mad at her?"

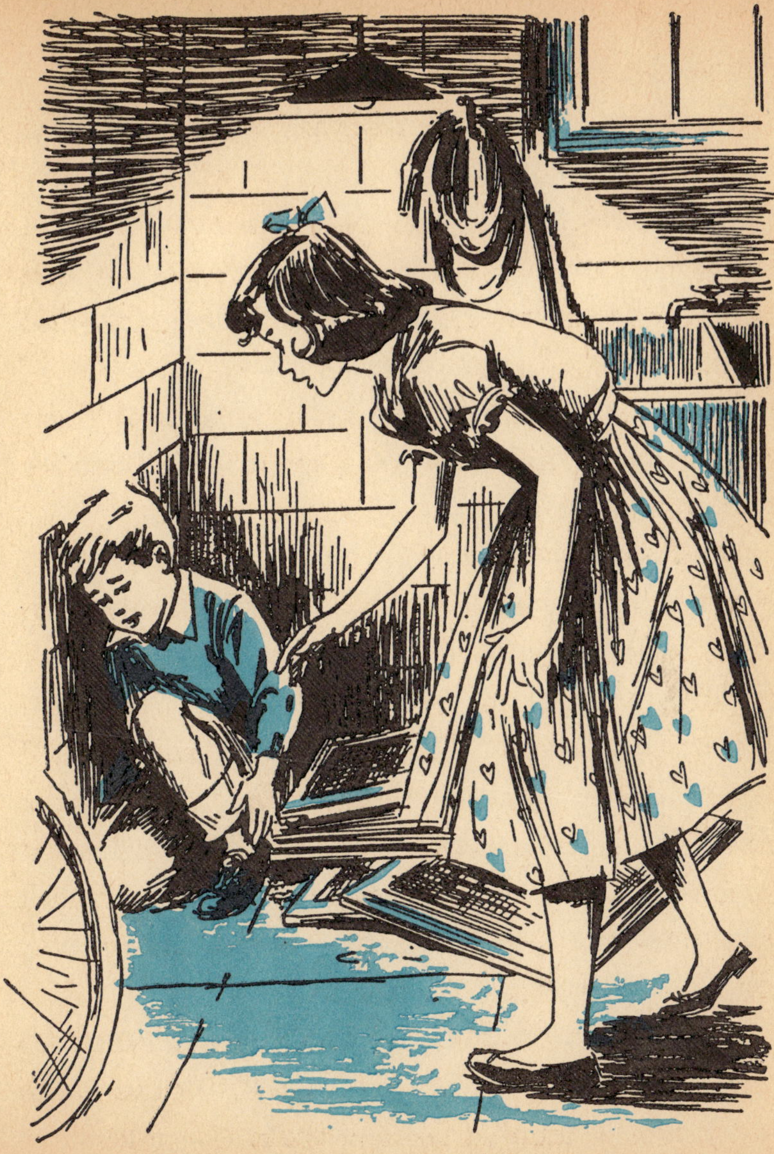

He nodded glumly. Donna sat him down on an old bench. "Look, Jimmy," she said softly, "we were wrong not to pay more attention to you this week. And we were wrong to make you go to places like Mitchells' without asking if you wanted to go. And we were very, very wrong not to ask you about the team today, when it was so important to you. And of course not getting you your dinner today was wrong, too."

Jimmy stared at the cellar floor. He would not look at his sister while she was talking.

"But as for that other thing," she continued, "why that's plain silly. I'm absolutely positive that Marjorie never said a word to Mr. Curtin about keeping you off the team."

"Cocoa's getting cold!" the teacher called down the cellar stairs.

"And I shall ask her so right now," Donna finished. "Come on, Jimmy. You'll feel better when you've had something to eat. And please forgive us."

Marjorie gasped when Donna told her what Jimmy had said about the team.

"Never, never, never," she said, shaking her head vehemently. "In fact, Jimmy, I'll tell you what I'll do. I'll ask Mr. Curtin why you didn't make the team—tactfully, of course. And I'll let you know right after school on Monday."

When the phone rang a few minutes later, Donna and Marjorie looked at each other.

"Oh, it's you, Mrs. Gray," Donna said. "Yes, he was here all the time. I'm awfully sorry we worried you. Thank you for calling."

"Well, the night ended happily after all," Donna said as she and Miss Dengrove turned off the lights. "Thanks again for the party, Margie."

They trudged wearily upstairs. Jimmy was already fast asleep.

"Now if only I didn't have to face Gladell in the morning," she thought, tossing her clothes in a heap on her chair. "I don't want to be around when she sees that mess downstairs."

CHAPTER 15   *Modern Methods*

"It's not only these messy paper plates, and those little dishes with gooey ice cream stuck to 'em," Gladell complained loudly, slamming a tray with dirty silverware on the kitchen counter.

"And it's not that there rug, that'll never get the creases out of it before your mamma gets home, Donna," she continued, hands on hips.

"And it's not even food all over the floor, like I have never seen in this house before," she went on, taking the broom and dust pan out of the kitchen closet. "Or even finger marks on the walls and heel marks on my nice varnished floors."

Donna put another load of dishes in the soapy water, trying not to hear.

Gladell shook her head sadly. "The minute I walked in

and saw bits of broken looking glass lyin' all over the front hall floor, I knew this was goin' to be a black day." She shook her head again and walked out of the kitchen. "A black day," she repeated mournfully.

"Oh, it was only a little bitty old mirror from somebody's purse," Donna said half to herself. "My goodness, did you ever see anybody so superstitious?"

What could possibly happen today? There were only a few things to be bought at the supermarket, and she and Marjorie had decided to shop after lunch. Yeeks, would she have to listen to Gladell go on like this all morning?

"All the parties your mamma has made for you, and this is the first time the house looked like a bunch of wild Indians was having a war dance in it." Gladell was back for the bucket and a cloth.

"Well, that's because the other parties were just for girls," Donna answered, "like that surprise party Mommy gave me for my birthday. But this one had boys, too, Gladell, and you just can't expect the place to look like nobody had been here."

"Humph!" Gladell snorted. "Bet the girls was almost as bad as the boys."

"They were—not," Donna finished weakly, remembering the oozy sundaes the girls had prepared, and the spirit with which they had stepped on balloons in the balloon dance. Actually, it was a wonder someone hadn't gotten cracked in the shins.

"We were just having fun," Donna said loyally. "Even Marjorie told me what nice boys and girls they were."

"I'm sure," the woman answered sarcastically. "Get any crowd of young people together these days and they all get crazylike. They may be nice when you take one or two at a time, but put 'em all together . . . ." She shook her head sadly and carried off the bucket of soapsuds.

Donna trailed her fingers in the dish pan. Maybe Gladell had something there, after all. When the whole gang got together, they did get sort of wild. Not like those juvenile delinquents you read about in the newspapers, but still—

"Maybe it was Gladell who saved me," she was to say to her mother later. Gladell, and that reflection in the mirror who kept reminding her about wanting to be just "one of the gang."

"A black day," came the refrain from the living room, accompanied by the sounds of scrubbing.

"Let's get out of here, Margie," Donna begged when she had finished in the kitchen.

"I've got to do some things for school." Miss Dengrove was working in her bedroom, to stay out of Gladell's way. "Besides, Jimmy said he had a tummyache, and he went back to bed. I'd better stay here with him."

"Is he really sick?" Donna asked with concern. "Do you think we should call a doctor?"

Marjorie smiled. "No, I think it's just the aftereffects of all the excitement yesterday. And now that there's no real reason for him to be out practicing baseball, he's got a sort of letdown feeling, I guess. Anyhow, he's asleep now and that'll do him more good than anything else."

"Well, if you don't mind, I think I'll go over to Ricky's for a while. I'll be back in time for lunch."

Ricky was delighted to see her, and to go over the events of the night before. Donna decided to skip the part about Jimmy. "It would look like we've been mistreating him or something," she thought.

"Do you really think it was that good?" she said, after listening to Ricky exclaim over the refreshments, the square dances, "and simply everything." It was so nice to hear these things. She musn't forget to tell Marjorie.

"Maybe my mother will let me give a party during Easter vacation," Ricky mused. "Would you help me plan it,

Donna?" The dark-haired girl nodded.

"Yeeks, I've got to run," she said. "Shopping this afternoon."

Ricky looked at her with envy. "You sound so grown-up, Donna. It must be wonderful to run a house without mothers and fathers nagging all the time, just as though it's your own house."

"Well, it's a responsibility," Donna answered solemnly. "But I'm getting on to it."

"Like the budget book," she thought, as she drove home from the supermarket with Marjorie. "I must remember to mark everything down that I spent this afternoon."

"Wasn't it nice that my baby-sitting money paid for practically the whole party?" she said to Miss Dengrove as they unloaded the packages from the car. "The house money just had to pay for things for the sandwiches."

"That reminds me, Donna." The teacher juggled a shopping bag and reached into her pocketbook. "You should put more money in the cooky jar, since I just cashed another check. That lone dollar bill has been sitting there all week."

"But—but where is it?" Donna thought in surprise when she looked into the jar. "Oh, dear, I simply must get something to use as a lid. Although a dollar couldn't simply *blow* out of here. Now what's happened this time?"

She looked in the budget book. No, the dollar should definitely be here.

"Marjorie"—now she could really talk to the teacher, for they knew each other so much better—"Marjorie, when was the last time you saw the dollar in the cooky jar?"

"Why, isn't it there?" The teacher put down the can of soup she was holding. "Now let me see. I'm sure it was there before I went to buy the ice cream yesterday, because I didn't remember how much money I had in my purse. But I know I didn't take it. Oh, dear, is it gone?"

Donna leaned one elbow on a counter. "Do you think, maybe...." She cocked her head toward the cellar, where Gladell was emptying the last bucket of dirty water. Come to think of it, the first time money had disappeared, hadn't Gladell been in the house?

Marjorie shook her head. "Oh, I'm sure that's not it, Donna. Nobody would just help themselves to someone else's money like that."

"You have more confidence in people than I do," Donna thought. Thank goodness she hadn't ever told Marjorie that she herself had been a suspect.

"Oh, I forgot to tell you, Donna." Gladell closed the cellar door behind her and called into the kitchen from the front hall. "You got a telephone call while you was gone. I wrote it down. And Jimmy said he was feelin' better, an' he went over to the Grays' for a little while. And did you get that there letter from India that come this afternoon? Guess it's from your folks."

"Thanks, Gladell." Donna gave the woman her check. "And we won't have any more parties, so you don't have to worry."

"I'm not worryin' about parties," Gladell muttered, tying her kerchief over her head. "It's that broken looking glass that worries me. A black day, that means. I'll be lucky if I don't get kilt goin' home. And you take care too, Donna."

"Now for Mommy's letter," Donna said, as she reached for the envelope. "You know, Margie, it seems as though they've been gone for years instead of a few weeks. Remember the snow when they left? Now it's almost Easter."

The Parkers were now traveling through South India and enjoying every bit of it. "You read it, too, Margie. Isn't that part about Trivandrum fascinating? I'll have to look it up on the map. Imagine being only a few degrees above the equator."

While Marjorie read the letter, Donna called Mrs. Payne, whose number Gladell had written down.

"Honestly, I'm constantly being amazed at these dinner invitations we keep getting, Margie," she said a few minutes later. "Can we go to the Paynes' on Monday night? Oh, dear, what about Jimmy? I guess he won't want to go."

But Jimmy, when he returned from the Grays', informed them that he had been invited to dinner at Skipper's house for that same evening.

"That's wonderful," Donna said. "You stay there until we call you, when we get home. We won't be late, Jimmy. Mrs. Payne said they eat early."

"Mother first met Dr. Payne when he talked to their study group," Donna told Marjorie during the drive late Monday afternoon. "And then he and his wife became good friends of Mommy and Daddy. Dr. Payne has all sorts of wonderful ideas about raising children. I only wish Mommy would listen to them."

"Like what?" Marjorie asked, stopping before an old brown-shingled house.

"Like not making children eat anything they don't want, and explaining the reasons for everything to them."

She rang the doorbell and waited. "He has two children and he says they're happy because he and his wife don't keep saying No." She rang the bell again.

A uniformed maid appeared at the door. "Doctor's not in," she announced and started to close the door.

"Is Mrs. Payne in?" Donna asked quickly. "I think she's expecting us."

The door opened, and the maid looked from Donna to Marjorie. "Won't you step in?" she said politely.

They followed her through what seemed to be Dr. Payne's waiting room, into a large, dim, old-fashioned living room.

"Mrs. Payne isn't in either," the maid said as she turned to leave them. "But I expect she'll be back soon. Just make yourselves comfortable."

Donna sat down on a brown leather sofa and looked around. "Maybe she had an errand to do," she said to Marjorie.

"She did say this Monday night, didn't she, Donna?" the teacher asked almost an hour later. The house seemed entirely empty. Not only were Dr. and Mrs. Payne out, and the children did not seem to be there, but there also were no sounds from the kitchen.

"The place seems haunted," Donna whispered. "It's almost dark in here now. Do you think we could turn on a light? Or should we just go home?"

As she reached for the lamp, the front door was opened. At the door to the living room stood Mrs. Payne wearing an astonished expression.

"I'm Donna Parker, and this is Marjorie Dengrove," Donna said after an awkward silence.

Mrs. Payne put down the child she was holding and laughed nervously.

"Oh, yes, Donna Parker, of course. Your mother and father are in Japan, aren't they? We do miss them, and I promised to keep an eye on you. You must tell us all about their trip. Here, dear"—she turned to the short, dark man who had followed her into the room and who was holding another child—"here, dear, take Nelson."

She removed her coat, and Donna saw that she was wearing a low-cut, sleeveless, blue lace dress. "Oh, this," she said, noticing Donna's expression. "We had to go to a wedding. I was so sorry we couldn't stay later, but we had to get home to give the children their dinner."

She turned to walk toward the kitchen, with Nelson now clinging to her skirts. "Will you join us for supper?"

Donna looked at Marjorie. But they had been asked for dinner, hadn't they?

"We'd love to," said Marjorie quickly. "Can I help you with the children? I guess you'll want to change out of that lovely dress."

"This?" The woman shrugged. "Oh, we never bother about clothes. In fact, I guess that's why the children are cranky. They've been wearing shoes all afternoon, and they're so confining!"

She kicked off her own shoes and the little boy followed suit. Donna pretended not to notice when Dr. Payne removed from the baby not only his shoes, but his socks, suit, and pants.

"There now," the doctor said with a smile. "Now he feels better, wearing just his undershirt. I always say modern parents wrap their children in far too many layers of clothes. Just see how happy he looks. I keep telling your mother's study group, Miss Parker—"

"Maybe the baby's happy," Donna thought, "but I'm not. I don't think it's very respectable to let a baby walk around with nothing on but an undershirt! And how he doesn't catch cold, I'll never know."

"Well, you can come out to the kitchen, if you like,"

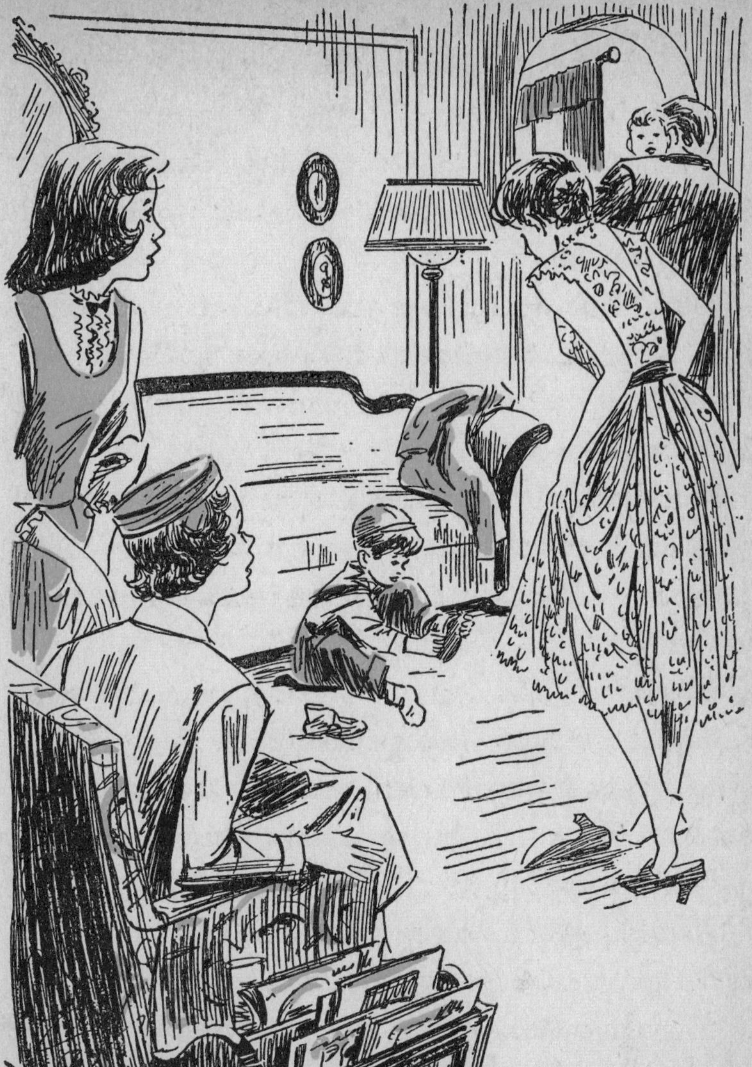

Mrs. Payne was saying to Marjorie. "But really, our meals are very simple."

"That's not quite the word," Donna thought wryly, as she sat down to a supper of sardines, cheese and crackers, and some leftover birthday cake. "It certainly doesn't seem to bother them, though."

It was true, Donna realized, that the children seemed happy. And not once did she hear either parent say No to a child.

When Nelson wanted more milk, he stood up in his chair and leaned across the table for it. When the baby ate a sardine—"Goodness, imagine giving a baby such indigestible food," Donna thought—he picked one up in his hand and shoved it in his mouth.

And when both children started to get noisy and irritable, Dr. Payne crooned, "Up to beddy-by, kiddies. Come with Daddy." And he picked up both children and left the room.

"Wouldn't you like to see them take their baths?" Mrs. Payne asked. "They're so sweet."

Donna and Marjorie followed her upstairs and had to watch the whole bath process.

"Yeeks!" Donna said, as she went to get the pairs of

pajamas Dr. Payne had forgotten. "Look at this room. Why, that little boy must have crayoned over every inch of wall as far up as he could reach."

"Isn't that interesting?" Mrs. Payne commented, coming in behind her. "Nelson is such a creative child. We certainly don't want to stifle him, the way most parents do. He gets such a feeling of expressing himself when he draws."

"Wow!" Donna exclaimed on the way home. "I wonder why they ever invited us. They certainly didn't seem prepared for company. If that's what she calls 'keeping an eye' on us!"

Then she giggled. "Did you ever see parents like that? You can be sure I'll never raise my children that way. And do you know," she turned to Marjorie, "I think maybe I'll even say No to them sometimes, even if it does make them unhappy. Why, I'd be ashamed to take children like that out in public."

"Sometimes appearances are important," Marjorie agreed. "The first night I came to dinner at your house, I was impressed with what good manners both you and Jimmy had."

They drove quietly for a while, and Donna's thoughts

roamed. There was that evening at the too-perfect house of the Mitchells, and now tonight at the far-from-perfect house of the Paynes.

"I don't know how Mommy and Daddy have done it," she thought with admiration, "but somehow they seem to have hit the middle course."

"Speaking of Jimmy's manners," Marjorie said as they neared the Parker house, "I think he feels better about the team now."

"Oh, did you talk to Mr. Curtin?" Donna asked.

The teacher nodded. "He told me that the only reason that Jimmy didn't make the team was"—her eyes twinkled—"was because the other boys were better ballplayers."

"Poor Jimmy! I bet he felt just dreadful."

"Not at all," Miss Dengrove replied. "He seemed to feel much better. Especially when I told him that Mr. Curtin said he'd give him some extra help."

"Oh, that was awfully nice of him," Donna said.

Miss Dengrove tooted the car horn in front of the Grays' house and Jimmy appeared at the front door.

"Coming in a minute," he called happily.

"Goodness! He seems like a different child," Donna said in amazement.

"Mr. Curtin also said that if Jimmy came to the Recreation Center ball field every day during the Easter vacation, he'd show him how to get better control—whatever that means. I guess he didn't realize at first how terribly upset Jimmy was when he didn't make the team."

"No wonder Jimmy looks so happy, getting all that extra attention," Donna said as she walked up the front steps. "It's wonderful of Mr. Curtin to give up part of his vacation to work with Jimmy."

"Yeeks!" she thought as she hung her coat in the hall closet. "Vacation! Why, Friday is the last day of school. The dance is on Saturday. And I haven't even gotten the rose taffeta dress from Ricky. Oh, why do I always leave everything for the last minute?"

CHAPTER 16 *Flowers and Dresses*

"I'll bring it over tomorrow after school," Ricky promised when Donna reminded her about the dress. "I'm sure it's come back from the cleaners by now."

"Order, order!" George Hart called. "This is practically our last meeting before the dance and we've got to tie up all the loose ends. First, the report from the music committee."

"We were allowed twenty dollars from the treasury to rent a juke box," Joyce Davenport said. "And we can still get one, if you want. But I just learned that for the same money, Richard White and his Jolly Juniors will play from eight thirty until eleven o'clock. I said I'd let them know by tonight."

"Richard White?" Donna whispered to Ricky. "Is that the same Richard who worked at Camp Three Pines when we were counselors at Cherrydale last summer?"

Ricky nodded. "They're just high school boys, but I hear the band has a great beat."

"Quiet!" called George, pounding on the desk. "How many think we should hire the band?"

Donna raised her hand along with almost everyone in the group. Oh, this would be fun. She hadn't seen Richard after the summer, because he now went to the senior high school. Would he remember her? Maybe he was going back to camp again and they would have more dates together.

The refreshment committee seemed to have things well in hand. "Not that it really matters," Donna thought. "Because everyone will want to go to the Sweet Shop afterwards anyhow."

"As for the decorations," Tommy Sheridan reported when his turn came, "our thanks go to Miss Donna Parker."

Donna looked up at the sound of her name. She really hadn't done anything at all since that letter to Mrs. Cunningham. In fact, Tommy had decided yesterday that, not having heard from Mrs. Cunningham, they would have to beg or borrow flowers from their parents and neighbors.

"Or use those same beaten-up old potted palms, and some crepe paper," Ricky had said, making a face.

"Donna knows all the right people," Tommy was saying now, "and George Hart, who signed the letter to a certain rich widow, received an answer just this morning." He waved a faintly perfumed piece of lavender stationery before them. "Here, this is what she says:

> Thank you so much for your charming letter. How wonderful that Donna Parker's class is having a little spring dance. Of course it must be the best, simply the best, that your school has ever had. She's such a lovely child. I shall be delighted to help in your decorating problem, and the idea of a spring garden sounds charming. Mike, my gardener, will be happy to supply you with tulips, daffodils, etc., since I shall be away at the time — Bermuda, I think.
>
> Sincerely,
> Stacey Cunningham
> (Mrs. John Q. X. Cunningham)

Tommy sat down, and everyone turned to Donna and

applauded. "To our *lovely child!*" called Jack Kingston.

"And if she's got even half the flowers you say," Ricky told her the next afternoon, "we'll really set this little old town on its ear."

"And here's the dress, Don," Ricky said, taking a paper cover off the hanger she had brought from her home. "Mother said all the spots have come out beautifully."

"Oh, it looks wonderful," Donna said delightedly.

"Try it on, Don," Ricky urged. "I'd love to see it on you again."

Donna could not resist the temptation. "Just for a second," she said. "I don't want to get it dirty."

"Here, help me, Rick," she called through the folds of material, her arms waving in the air.

"It—it seems a little tight," Ricky said. "Was it this hard to get into before?"

Donna shook her head, which emerged slightly tousled from the exertion.

"The sleeves seem tight, too," she said in an unbelieving tone. "Wait till I get it zipped up the side."

"Oh, Donna!" Ricky took several steps backward. "It doesn't even begin to close. And look at how short it is! The whole dress shrank!"

Donna stood helplessly in the center of the room.

"The cleaning," she said. "It shrank in the cleaning. Oh, Ricky, what'll I do now?" The dress was past repair.

"Are you sure you don't have anything you could wear?" Ricky asked, putting her head into Donna's closet.

"You can look if you want to, but I know," Donna answered mournfully.

"Well, I guess you could wear a skirt and blouse," Ricky offered. "Or one of your cottons from the summer."

"You forget, Rick. We were at camp all summer and Mommy didn't make me any new ones. And the ones from the year before are all too small. Of course, I *could* wear that fancy white formal that Uncle Roger gave to me. But I won't do it," she added with determination. "Either I go dressed the way the other girls are, or I stay home."

"Oh, Donna!" Ricky picked at the mane of the old stuffed animal on the bed. "You can't stay home. It wouldn't be a party without you."

"Something wrong, girls?" Marjorie stood at the doorway. "You both look so glum."

Donna pointed to the rose dress and said, "It shrank."

"Nothing else to wear?" Marjorie asked.

Ricky and Donna shook their heads in unison.

"Well, then," Marjorie said brightly. "We'll just have to buy you a new dress."

The two girls looked up. Then Donna leaned back. "With what?" she asked.

"I can lend you the money," Marjorie decided, "and you can pay me back when you earn it."

Donna jumped up and hugged her. She could always baby-sit for Mrs. Williams, who had been so disappointed when she explained that she would have to stop for a while. "Oh, Margie, you're a doll, a real doll. Can we look for one tomorrow right after school? There's that cute little Sub-Teen Shop, where I've always wanted to get a dress. But you know, Mommy makes all my clothes—"

"Humph!" Ricky sniffed when Marjorie had left. "Such generosity! She'll be lending you the money that she took from the cooky jar, I'll bet!"

"Ricky!" Donna turned fiercely. "Don't you say such a thing about Marjorie. She never took a penny out of that cooky jar. I'm as sure of that as I am of my own name."

"Then what happened to it?" Ricky demanded. "Even after your party, there was that dollar bill that just vanished. How do you explain that?"

"I don't know," Donna answered hotly. "But some day

I'll find out, and then you'll be sorry you said such things about a friend of mine, Ricky West."

"Well!" Ricky stood up. "Maybe she's a better friend to you than I am. Maybe your precious Marjorie Dengrove will walk you to school every morning. I'm leaving!" And with that she flounced out of the room and down the stairs.

"Oh, she'll get over it, Donna," Marjorie said the next day, on the way to the Sub-Teen Shop. "Gracious, I remember all the little quarrels I used to have with my best friend, and we always made up in a day or two. Wait'll she sees you in your fancy new dress."

"No, not velveteen—that's for winter," Donna said to the salesgirl. "And not wool, either. Don't you have anything that's simple, but dressy, to wear to a school dance?"

"Now what?" Donna asked as they stood outside the shop. "That was a fine suggestion—to come back after Easter when the spring dresses arrive. The dance is in two more days!"

"There are lots more stores," Marjorie consoled her. "And we made an early start this afternoon. We'll get a dress for you if we have to go to New York!"

Hours later, Donna sat in the car and rubbed the backs of her legs. "What was that about New York, Margie? It seems like we've been halfway there and back again, and still no dress."

"Imagine!" Miss Dengrove shook her head. "All those stores, in every town for miles around, and not one of them with a dress for you."

"Now what do we do?" Donna asked.

"We still have tomorrow," Marjorie replied. "There must be places to look that we haven't been to yet."

"It was sweet of you to try so hard," said Donna the next day on the way home, after their shopping trip had failed again. "I really feel awfully bad, making you drive so far and dragging you in and out of all those stores."

Marjorie shook her head and squeezed the girl's hand.

"It just doesn't seem possible, Donna. I didn't realize that girls your age were so hard to dress. Why, I just walk into the junior department of any store—" She stopped in the middle of the sentence and looked at Donna.

"Come on," she said, turning sharply into a side street. "Oh, me, oh, my, if it only works!"

"What, what? Tell me!" Donna tugged at the teacher's elbow. "Where are we going?"

"To my old boarding house. After the snowstorm I took most of my things to your house, but I left a few that I knew I'd never wear. Now you keep your fingers crossed," she called as she ran up the steps of a small white house.

"Ooh, I can't wait," Donna said, as Marjorie reappeared in a few moments.

"It's really awfully cute," Marjorie explained as Donna held the dress up in the car. "It's very tailored, almost shirtwaist style. But the flowered taffeta material makes it quite dressy, and I have a wide pink belt that you can wear with it, if it fits."

"Perfect!" Donna sighed, looking at herself in her mother's bedroom mirror a little later. "Oh, Margie, you've saved my life again. I never knew we wore the same size, did you?"

"We-ell," Marjorie held her fingers to her lips thoughtfully. "It's quite long. But we could take up the hem."

"If you mark it, I'll do the sewing," Donna volunteered. "I've been enough trouble to you already."

"First thing tomorrow morning," Marjorie agreed. "We'd better get dinner ready now, or Jimmy will hide in the cellar again," she laughed.

"Ready now?" Marjorie called as Donna was finishing

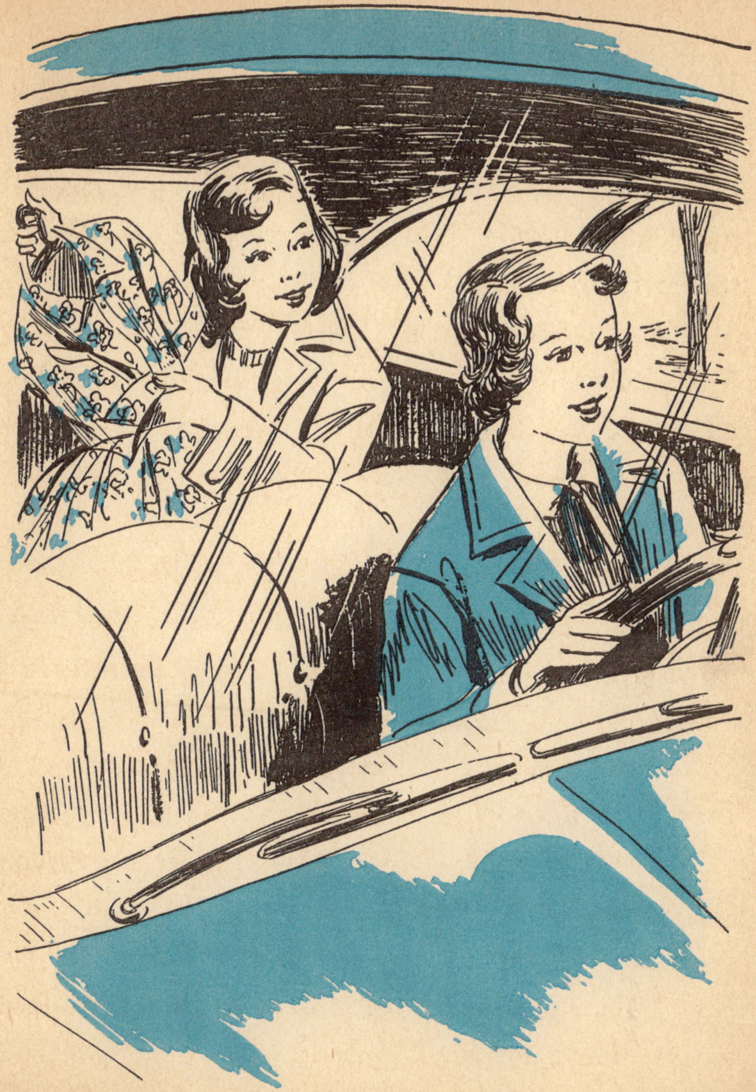

the breakfast dishes the next morning. "I've got the pins in the living room."

"Why, here come Tommy and Jack Kingston and—and Ricky," Donna said, as she turned slowly on the paper-covered coffee table and looked out the living-room window. "I wonder what they want."

"Hi!" said the boys as Marjorie, her mouth full of pins, went to open the front door. "Hi, Donna. Can you come with us?"

"Where?" Donna asked, as Marjorie resumed her measuring and pinning.

"Out to Mrs. Cunningham's," Tommy replied. "Nobody could drive us out, so we thought we'd go out on our bicycles. We can get the flowers and put them in the baskets. It's going to take us a long time to decorate the gym, you know."

Donna looked down at Marjorie. "Gee, I wish I could go, too, and I'm sorry Miss Dengrove can't drive us out. But we've just got to finish this hem. I don't know how long it will take me, but the minute I'm through I'll go down to the gym and help with the decorating."

"Oh, that's all right," Jack Kingston said. "You got the flowers for us, and that was the hardest job of all."

As they turned to leave, Ricky, who had been standing quietly by, said, "The dress looks nice, Donna."

"I guess that means she's not mad any longer," Donna said to the top of Marjorie's head.

"Well, I'm getting mad," Marjorie mumbled. "Every time you move, the hem looks different. If the skirt weren't so full—"

Finally the pinning was completed to her satisfaction. "I'll have to hurry," Donna thought. "It'll take hours to baste and hem a skirt so wide, and I really should help with the decorating."

But by the time Donna arrived at the school, most of the flowers had been arranged.

"Oh!" Donna looked around in amazement. It was hard to believe that this magnificent bower of blossoms was the stuffy old gym where they played volleyball and did exercises.

"Do you like it? We're not quite through," Tommy said proudly.

"It's—just unbelievable. It's gorgeous!" she murmured "I don't think I've ever seen so many flowers at one time. And you've done such a terrific job of arranging them."

"Oh, everybody helped," said Tommy, anxious to share

the credit. "The idea of covering the basketball baskets with tulips was Anne's. And Karen made that sort of forest effect in the corner over there with bushes and those little birch trees."

Bushes! Trees! She had had no idea that Mrs. Cunningham would be as generous as all that. Oh, well, the bushes probably were ready for planting. The roots were covered with burlap and seemed well-protected. Certainly Mike knew what he was doing.

"How did you ever carry them all here on your bikes?" Donna asked.

"Well," Tommy explained, "Sally Graham finally got her brother who has a car, and he helped a lot. And do you know, when we got back to school, Mrs. Cunningham had had somebody deliver a lot *more* flowers?" He shook his head. "Boy, Donna, that woman doesn't do things halfway, does she? When she said this should be the best dance the junior high ever had, she really meant it, didn't she? Just wait'll everyone sees it tonight."

"I'll bet they'll be talking about this dance for years," Donna said. She had no idea how true her words were.

CHAPTER 17 *The Dance*

"Oh, the gym is just scrumptious, Margie," Donna said when she returned. "I wish you could come tonight."

"I wish I could too, honey. But I'm baby-sitting, remember? You've got a little brother, you know, and speaking of your family, a letter just arrived for you. From Paris!"

"Yeeks!" Donna shouted, racing for the letter. "How wonderful! I forgot that Mommy and Daddy are supposed to come home right after Easter. Time has simply flown!"

She looked at the teacher. "And then you'll have to go back to that old boarding house, won't you? Oh, I wish there were more room here, and you could stay forever."

"Thanks, sweetie. Hadn't you better open your letter?"

"Oh, oh, oh!" Donna danced up and down. "Margie, Margie! They're going to be home on Tuesday, this very next Tuesday. Isn't that wonderful!"

"You'd better let me read it." Marjorie took the letter from the girl, who was waving it about, and began to read:

> We were able to leave India a few days early, which was very lucky because the temperature was almost 105°, and quite uncomfortable. And then when we got to Paris, we collapsed. We hadn't realized how exhausted we were. So instead of spending a week in a Paris hotel room, we decided to take the boat back tomorrow morning and relax on the trip home. We'll be arriving in New York on Tuesday. Since school is out, perhaps Miss Dengrove could bring you and Jimmy to meet us at the pier. Then Miss Dengrove could have at least a few days of her vacation free.
> See you soon. Be good.
> Love,
> Mother and Daddy

"Oh, Margie!" Donna cried. "Could we? Could we really go to New York?"

"I think so," the teacher smiled. "It's always exciting to watch the big ocean liners dock. Now you'd better run, honey. You still have to press your dress while I get dinner."

"How will you get to school tonight?" Marjorie asked while they were eating. "You don't have dates for a dance like this, do you?"

Donna shook her head and swallowed a bite of bread and butter. "No, not real dates. We go in—in sort of little groups. Tommy and Jack Kingston and Ricky and I will all go together, and Mrs. Sheridan said she'd pick us up about eight o'clock."

"And how about getting home?"

"Oh, one of the other mothers will call for us at the Sweet Shop after the dance. We're all going there afterwards." She pushed her chair back. "No dessert for me tonight, Margie, please. And I'll do all the dishes tomorrow." For Marjorie had offered to do the dinner dishes by herself.

"I'm almost ready," came the call from upstairs when a car honked outside promptly at eight. "Oh, Margie"— Donna paused for a moment, breathless, in front of the hall mirror—"do you think I look all right?"

"Gorgeous!" said Marjorie, and even Jimmy gave a wolf whistle as he caught a glimpse of his sister.

"Have fun!" the teacher called, as Donna disappeared down the steps carrying the white wool jacket Miss Dengrove had lent her.

"Oh, I am having fun," Donna thought, every few minutes during the evening.

She knew she looked her best. Marjorie's dress was just right. "I would have felt awful in Uncle Roger's white dress," she thought, looking at the one girl who was wearing a low-cut, long net gown.

The band was amazingly good, and much better to dance to than records on a juke box. Richard had recognized her immediately.

"I thought that was you, Donna," he said during an intermission, coming up to join her near the punch bowl. "But you've grown up so much, I hardly knew you."

He was still as handsome as he had been last summer, and she felt quite important talking to the leader of the band, an *older boy*.

"Oh," she answered coolly, half turning away, "I thought you'd forgotten all about me. Camp was so long ago . . . ."

Richard fiddled with his tie. "Well, senior high school is a lot more work than junior high," he said. "And then we organized this band so we could earn a little money, and I've—I've just been awfully busy. But I have been meaning to call you," he finished with a rush.

Donna turned her most winning smile on him. "I think the band is just wonderful, Richard. Oh, they seem to be getting back on the stand. I guess you'd better go."

"Guess so," he nodded. "But I really will call you, Donna. Maybe next week, during vacation."

"Oh," Donna thought, as she watched him disappear into the crowd, "I forgot to tell him that I'm going to New York on Tuesday!" She went to put her cup down next to the punch bowl.

"If it isn't Donna Parker, rosy and blooming again," said Mrs. Thomas, coming toward her. "You look a lot better than you did a few weeks ago when you came into my office."

"Maybe it's the dress," Donna said, curtsying demurely in return for the compliment. "This is my best color."

"And maybe it's those extra hours of sleep you've been getting. No more baby-sitting, eh, Donna?" The dean of girls nodded wisely.

"Oh—uh—don't you think the gym looks nice?" Donna asked, trying to change the subject.

"Beautiful, simply beautiful," Mrs. Thomas agreed. "And I hear you're the girl who's responsible."

"Indeed she is," said George Hart, coming up to join them. "Weren't we lucky she knew Mrs. Cunningham?"

"Mrs. Cunningham must be a very generous person," Mrs. Thomas commented. "That was a lovely letter that she wrote, George, saying she would give the class the flowers for the dance."

"Did you see that little forest effect that Karen made in the corner of the gym?" he asked. Mrs. Thomas turned to look, and George whispered, "Come on, Donna, let's dance."

"This place is loaded with teachers," he said, as they excused themselves to Mrs. Thomas. "And believe me, they're impressed with the way the place looks. No professional decorator could have done a better job than our own class members. The school will never forget us, Donna."

"And I'll never forget tonight," she thought happily, as she went to get her jacket at the end of the evening. "I danced every single dance. And everyone made such a fuss over me, just because I know Mrs. Cunningham."

She joined the others in her group, and they walked the few short blocks to the Sweet Shop.

"Looks like everyone's going in the same direction," Jack said. "We'd better hurry or we won't get a booth!"

"Over here, over here," called Anne Franklin and George Hart, waving to them from a booth at the back of the store. The juke box was blaring away, and there were so many boys and girls milling about that it took them several minutes to join Anne and George.

"Hurry up and order," Anne said. "There's only one waitress, and she doesn't know whether she's coming or going. Ooh, look, here's the rest of the gang."

With much squeezing and pushing, they made room for Mary Jefferson and Karen, but Steve Collins and Bill Blanchard were forced to stand up.

"And here come Sally Graham and Joyce Davenport, and all the rest," said Anne. "Can't we get another booth?"

"Find seats, find seats," boomed the manager, edging his way through the crowd. "Fire laws, you know."

"Well, my goodness!" said Sally, as the man moved past them. "Why doesn't he get seats for us, then? I don't like to stand, either. After all, we're the most important members of the class, aren't we?"

"Sure are!" said Steve, clapping Bill on the back. "Who pedaled those bikes all the way to Cunningham's Classy Cottage?"

"We did!" they answered in unison, and Donna giggled.

"And who risked life and limb getting up on those stepladders, so the blossoms could bloom where blossoms never bloomed before?" called Anne Franklin.

"We did!" The answer came back louder. Donna's eyes sparkled. Oh, she wished she could have helped, too, instead of having to stay home to sew a hem.

"And who planned this whole dance anyhow, and worked and slaved day after day!"

"We did!" came the roar. The other people in the Sweet Shop were looking at them. Oh, wasn't it wonderful to be part of such a marvelous group of boys and girls, the center of everything!

"George did!" Tommy protested weakly. Everyone laughed until they were almost sick.

"Good old George!" someone said. "Good old Donna!" someone else said.

"King George!" a boy called.

"Queen Donna!" a girl's voice said—Donna thought it was Ricky's.

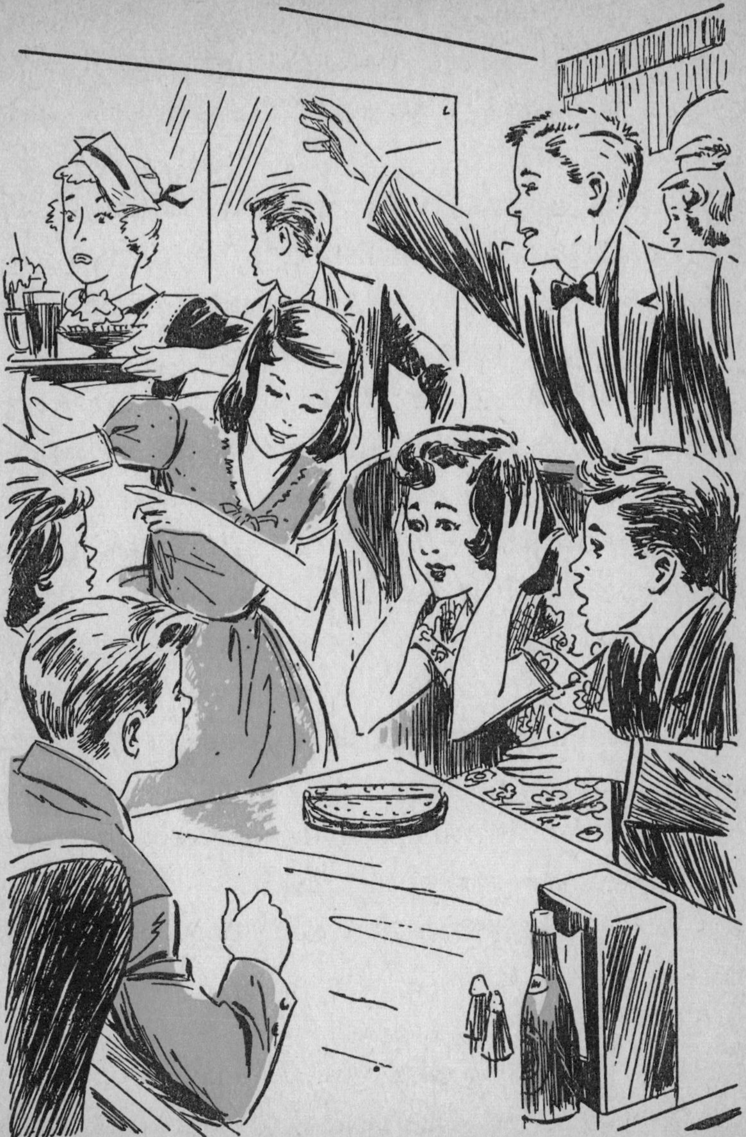

"Let's crown them!" The suggestion caught on.

"With napkins!"

"No, with soup bowls."

"I anoint thee with ketchup," Jack said, holding a bottle over George's head.

"Hey, wait a minute!" George ducked in time, and the ketchup streamed down on the table top.

Donna helped mop it up with her napkin.

"Orders, please," said the harassed waitress.

"Hamburgers and cokes for everyone!" George called out. "Okay, gang?"

"Have some salt for your hamburger," Ricky called to Karen, sliding the salt shaker to the other end of the table.

"Have some pepper!" Mary called. "Oops!" For she had pushed the pepper shaker a little too hard and it had gone over the edge of the table and crashed on the floor.

The rest of the crowd in the little restaurant was beginning to thin out.

"Ooh, seats!" Sally squealed, sliding into the booth next to Donna's.

"Here comes the food!" Bill Blanchard announced. "Give the lady some room!"

The waitress, her face flushed and her cap askew, set the

crowded tray down on the table.

"Cokes coming up!" Bill called again, as the manager appeared carrying the drinks.

"To the most successful dance that little old Summerfield Junior High ever had!" toasted Steve Collins.

"To us!" they toasted back.

"How about some mustard?" someone asked.

"Mustard! Mustard!" The cry went up.

Joyce found a jar of mustard on another table and brought it back with her.

"Would you like it with hamburger, or with ketchup?" someone asked, grabbing the mustard bottle and pouring the ketchup into it.

"Hey, hey!" The manager was glowering at them. "Whaddaya think yer doing? I never saw such a bunch of wild, noisy kids in my life. What kinda place d'ya think yer in, anyhow?"

The noise decreased.

"Ya don't come from Summerfield, do ya? Summerfield kids got better manners. Come on, come on. Finish watcha got and get outta here. And don't come back again, hear me?"

The manager pounded on the table and stalked away.

There was complete silence, as the boys and girls looked at each other.

"Why, of all the nerve!" Karen whispered. "Imagine, talking to us that way!"

"Who does he think he is?" Bill muttered.

"Saying we're not from Summerfield, just because we were having a good time," Ricky said softly.

"Why, we *are* Summerfield!" Donna thought, "at least, we're the most important members of the graduating class of the junior high school."

Standing on her front porch a little later, and waving to her friends as Tommy's mother drove away, she heard the echo of Gladell's voice. "Get any crowd of young people together nowadays, and they all get crazy-like. One or two at a time may be nice...."

Why was it? Donna thought. Why had they acted like that—noisy and silly and disgracefully rude—when they were usually such nice boys and girls? And she had been as bad as the rest. Just because she wanted to be one of the group. That reflection in the mirror had warned her, and she had paid no heed. She would really be too ashamed ever to walk into the Sweet Shop again.

The next morning, when she was awakened by Marjorie

shaking her, saying, "Donna, there's a policeman downstairs, and he wants to talk to you," she sat bolt upright in her bed. Last night at the Sweet Shop! Some one had reported their behavior to the police!

The policeman, however, did not question her about the Sweet Shop at all. He wanted information about something far more serious.

CHAPTER 18   *Home Again*

"But we got permission from Mrs. Cunningham, Officer," Donna said, now fully awake. She pulled her bathrobe tighter around her and looked at Marjorie. The teacher seemed as perplexed as she was by the questioning. "In fact, George Hart has the letter she wrote saying that Mike would give us the flowers for the dance."

"Ah, ha!" The policeman pointed his finger at her. "And did ye know that Mike's sister got sick, and he was called to go and stay with her? And here it was the day off for the cook and that other fellow—"

"Foster," Donna supplied.

"That's him. And Mike so worried about not bein' there when you kids came, and you not gettin' the flowers Mrs. Cunningham had promised. So what did he do but give all the flowers to Foster to deliver at the high school on his way in to town. And Foster swears he delivered them."

"Oh, then those were the flowers Tommy found when he got back to the gym." She clapped her hand over her mouth. "But who was at the Cunningham estate to tell the committee which flowers to take?"

"Ah, ha!" Again the policeman pointed at her as though she were well on the way to solving a complicated mystery story. "That's the point! There was exactly no one home. Those kids just helped themselves—took whatever they fancied, and plenty of it, too. And when that gardener called the station this morning, to report what had happened, he sounded like he was going to have a heart attack any minute."

"But the little birch trees! And the forsythia bushes! And all those tulips and daffodils!" Donna was aghast.

The officer shook his head sadly. "And some of them mighty rare specimens, too, from what the gardener said. Well, I can see you don't know much about it, miss. Sorry to have bothered you, but Mr. Greer gave us your name along with the rest of the dance committee."

"Marjorie, Marjorie." Donna looked at the teacher, whose face was as pale as her own. The officer picked up his cap and left.

"The whole town will know about it. And I can imagine how upset Mr. Greer and the teachers are. What do you think will happen? Do—do you think anyone will go to jail?" Donna whispered. "Oh, it's all my fault. If I only hadn't told Ricky about the greenhouse—if I only—" But how could they have done it? Gone to a stranger's house and just helped themselves?

If she had been with them, would she have joined them? After last night at the Sweet Shop, she wasn't sure. Just last night she had been so sorry to have had to stay home to work on Marjorie's dress. But it was the luckiest thing that had ever happened to her. Probably they just hadn't stopped to think.

Which was just what Ricky said when she spoke to her on the telephone.

"After all, we did have permission," Ricky said. "And no one was there to tell us what to do. Gee, Donna, it certainly didn't seem wrong at the time. I know we're awfully sorry, and I also know that being sorry won't put the flowers back." Her voice dropped to a whisper. "What—what do you think will happen to us?"

The evening paper on Monday asked the same question. When the leading members of the graduating class did something so shocking, the editorial said, parents certainly would have to take action. It was a disgrace to all of Summerfield.

"Our parents had a meeting," Ricky reported by phone to Donna later that night. "Oh, why did this have to happen just before Easter vacation? No parties, no gatherings, no *nothing* all during the holiday," she finished ungrammatically and mournfully.

"I feel as though I should be punished, too," Donna thought as she undressed. How could she face her own parents the very next day? What a way to welcome them home!

"Now cheer up," Marjorie consoled her the next morning as they parked the car at the station. "You're not going to look so weepy all the way to New York, are you? After all, you didn't do anything wrong, Donna."

"I feel so—so responsible, though, Marjorie. But I don't think we ought to mention it until Mother and Daddy have been home for a while, do you?" She hated the prospect of telling them about Mrs. Cunningham's flowers.

"Hey, quit talkin' so much," Jimmy called. "The train'll be here in a minute."

"Imagine going to New York again, so soon after our

press convention. Gee, it seems as though that was only last week," Donna mused. "But look at all the things that have happened in that time." India had only been a place on the map to her then. Now her mother and father had spent a whole month there, and she was going to meet the ocean liner that was bringing them home.

The crowd waiting at the pier was already large, but the gates were locked.

"Can't we even go up the gangplank?" Jimmy complained. "This'll prob'ly be my only chance to be on a boat this big."

"We can't even get into Customs," Donna said.

Jimmy looked at his sister blankly.

"Customs," she repeated. "That's where government inspectors look at your baggage to see that you're not bringing in things like dope or stolen jewelry."

Jimmy looked disgusted. "Aw, they know Mom and Dad would never do things like that."

"They also have to pay duty," added Miss Dengrove, laughing. "That's a sort of tax on all the things they bought abroad."

"Ooh, boy," Jimmy squealed. "I almost forgot about that. What do you suppose they brought us, Sis? Hey, I'm goin' to ask that man if we can't go in."

"Jimmy, no!" Donna called as the little figure squirmed through the crowd. But a minute later, Jimmy turned and beckoned to them.

"Just stick with me," the boy said importantly. "I explained who we were and the man said we could go in. He said they'd be standing near a sign that said *P,* for Parker."

Jimmy dashed one way and Donna another, each wanting to be the first to greet the new arrivals. Past piles of luggage Donna went, past straw baskets and wooden trunks and boxes and bales and cartons and hatboxes, past customs inspectors examining suitcases, and past men and women sorting their belongings.

"Donna," a voice called softly from behind her.

The girl turned. A few feet away, an elegant woman stood beside several suitcases. She was hatless and wore a bright chiffon scarf at the neckline of her black coat. It was —it couldn't be—

"Mother!" she cried breathlessly, and ran to fling her arms around Mrs. Parker's neck.

"You went right past me," Mrs. Parker laughed, hugging her daughter.

"You—you look so different, Mommy." Donna moved a step away and looked again. "You look like a—a real world-traveler!"

"And here comes Jimmy," Mrs. Parker said, as her son tumbled into her arms. "Here comes Daddy with the customs inspector, too. We'll be out of here in a few minutes now, I think." She sighed. "My, it's good to see you again."

There were hilarious greetings for Mr. Parker, too.

Miss Dengrove stood shyly by. Mrs. Parker turned to her. "Thank you so much for bringing the children to meet us. Are you all worn out from these six weeks?"

"No indeed," the teacher replied. "The children were wonderful, and we had a grand time."

"And Mr. Curtin is helping me with my baseball!" Jimmy broke in.

"But we want to hear about *you*," Donna interrupted. "All about the trip, and the people, and everything."

The entire ride from New York to Summerfield was a jumble of talking. Not once did a story get finished, for someone was always reminded of something else to tell.

"Oh, dear me," Mrs. Parker said when their car stopped at the Parker house. "It's going to take weeks to get all the stories sorted out. But there's something that can be sorted

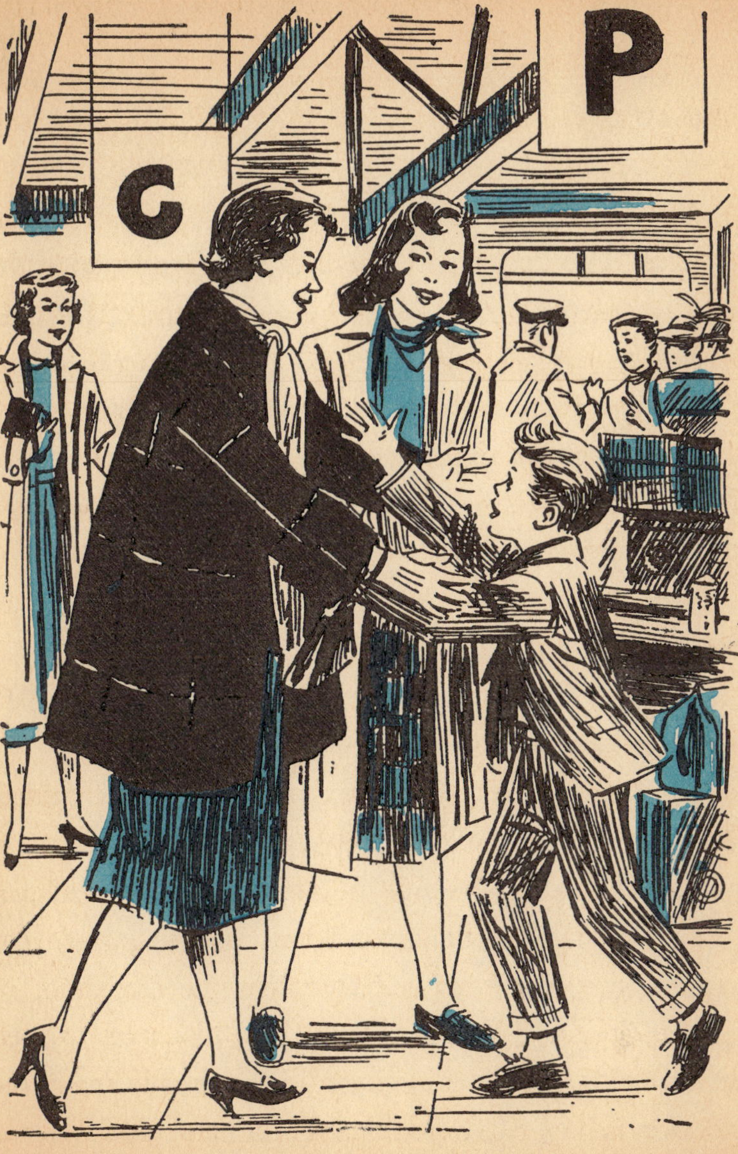
G
P

out right away, and that's the souvenirs we brought back with us."

"Yowie!" Jimmy shouted. "Presents! Come on, everybody."

"They're really just little things," Mr. Parker said. "We sent home by ship from Madras most of the larger things we bought there, because excess baggage from Madras to Paris by air costs almost fourteen dollars a pound! But I think we brought a little remembrance for every member of the family—that is, everyone but Donna's dove."

Jimmy giggled. "Some member of the family!"

Donna bit her lip. Goodness, she hadn't even looked at the dove since the excitement about the dance. And if her mother saw a dirty cage, she would feel that Donna still had to be nagged and scolded to get things done.

"We can unpack in my bedroom," Mrs. Parker said, as they hung their coats in the hall closet. "All the presents are in that small brown bag." She looked around. "My, it's good to be home again. Everything looks so lovely. We didn't realize what a nice home we have, did we, Sam?"

"I didn't either," thought Donna. "And I learned it right here in Summerfield, visiting people like the Mitchells and the Paynes." But how could you tell your own parents that they were the ones who had made their home what it was? It would sound so—so sticky.

"I'll be up in a minute, Mommy. You go ahead," Donna said. She would simply have to clean the cage before her mother saw it.

Thank goodness she had come back to the kitchen before her mother did. Because there was the dove, sitting in its favorite place on top of the cupboard.

"I guess I forgot to close the cage door again," Donna thought, "and now that the weather is warmer we keep forgetting to close the kitchen door, too."

Hands on hips, she stood and looked up at the dove. "Come on now, you stupid old bird," she muttered. "I don't have time for any nonsense today. Get down here *at once.*"

"Hey, Don, c'mon," Jimmy called from the steps. "Whatcha doin' in there?"

"Just a second," she called back. If she stood on a chair, could she reach the bird? No, she knew from past experience that it wouldn't work.

The broom! That would do it. She ran to get it and made a quick sweep over the top of the cupboard. The dove, annoyed by the movement, uttered a loud squawk and flew off. But Donna did not lunge toward the bird. She stood absolutely still.

For, fluttering down from the top of the cupboard were several pieces of green paper. They were much clawed and torn, but it was still obvious that they had once been—money!

Bills! Every one that had been missing! The five-dollar bill that had disappeared right after the snowstorm, and the dollar that she had blamed Jimmy for, and the money that was lost just before the party, and the money that was missing after the party—why, that one sweep of the broom had brought them all tumbling down!

Donna stood there, staring. "You dreadful, mischievous little bird!" she thought. "Do you know all the trouble you caused me? All the sleepless nights? Do you know you made me suspicious of my own family and of my best friends?"

Poor Miss Dengrove! How unjustly she had been accused, if only in thought.

Then Donna squared her shoulders. After all, she had realized long before the money came fluttering down that Marjorie could have had nothing to do with the disappearing bills.

"I guess that's what Mommy calls her 'womanly intuition,'" she thought. "Just a feeling that you can't describe but you know is right. As soon as I get a chance, I'll have to tell Mommy and Daddy all about it. Wasn't it lucky that I never said anything to Marjorie? I'd never have been able to face her again."

She scooped up the handful of green papers and stuffed them into her skirt pocket. After things had calmed down a little, she would have to go back and figure out what had happened each time. Come to think of it, hadn't Marjorie told her that Anne had let the bird out of its cage during the party? She just hadn't looked at the cooky jar afterwards, or she would have noticed it immediately.

Donna took a deep breath. As she put the dove back into its cage she smiled slightly. Mother and Daddy were home safely; the money was found; everything was turning out beautifully.

As she dashed up the steps to her parents' bedroom, the telephone rang.

The police! The flowers! She had almost forgotten. Oh, dear, everything was still far from all right.

"I'll get it," she called, rushing down the steps again, her heart beating furiously.

"Long distance," the operator said.

Donna's jaw dropped. "But Mommy and Daddy are *here*," she thought wildly.

"For a Miss Marjorie Dengrove. Bermuda calling," the operator continued.

"Bermuda?" Marjorie repeated a few seconds later. "Could it possibly be Mrs. Cunningham?" she whispered to Donna.

Donna shivered. Surely Mrs. Cunningham wouldn't blame Marjorie for what had happened.

"It was my fault, Margie," Donna said tearfully. "Please tell her it was all my fault. And please—please ask her not to send anyone to jail. We'll make it up to her somehow if she'll give us a chance."

The conversation between Mrs. Cunningham and Marjorie was short, and the teacher's end, which consisted mainly of "Of course" and "But—" conveyed nothing. But when Miss Dengrove put down the telephone she was wearing a broad smile.

"You'll never guess, Donna," she said. "Oh, this is just wonderful. I'm going to have a real vacation, after all."

"What's this about a vacation?" Mr. Parker asked, coming down the steps.

"Mrs. Cunningham just called," Marjorie explained, "and insists that I fly to Bermuda this evening. She says she's awfully bored there and she'd like some company. She has my ticket ready at the airline office and she wants me to come as her guest. What's more," Marjorie turned to Donna, "I won't have to go back to my boarding house, either. She says she'd appreciate it very much if, after the holiday, I stay at her house. In fact, she acted as though I'd be doing her a favor! And she said it was her fault about the flowers, because no one was at home."

Mr. and Mrs. Parker looked at each other, bewildered. "I'm sure," commented Mr. Parker, "you two girls know what this is all about, but it sounds like Greek—or should we say Hindi—to me."

"Margie, is that all she said about the flowers, honestly?" asked Donna.

"Well," the teacher said, "she did say that she realized how badly the children must feel, and perhaps they could come and help Mike plant the new flowers."

"Could they!" Donna breathed. "They'd be delighted. And of course, I'll come, too. Because, after all, I was the cause of it all."

"For that matter, I was, too," Marjorie laughed. "And

I'll be there to see that you all work hard." She cracked an imaginary whip in the air.

"Hey!" Jimmy called from the upstairs hall. "How long do I have to wait? I can't even get the suitcase open, Mom," he complained.

"A good thing, too, my boy," said his father, taking the steps two at a time. "Goodness knows what would be left by now if you had actually opened it."

Donna sat on the floor, between Marjorie and her mother, while Mr. Parker handed out packages and Jimmy raced excitedly back and forth. It was almost like Christmas.

Indian dolls, sandalwood carvings, rosewood elephants, ivory figurines, silk scarfs, were presented with numerous *oohs* and *aahs*.

But Donna could scarcely keep her mind on the gifts, even when she was given her first bottle of real French perfume from Paris. Her mind was too busy with a multitude of other things.

It was almost too much for one day. The trip to New York, the wonderful sight of her parents again, finding the money, the arrangement about the flowers, even the problem about Marjorie's boarding house solved.

What could the future possibly hold that would be as

exciting as these past six weeks had been?

Of course, the next six weeks would be busy with preparations for graduation, with exams and rehearsals and getting ready for senior high. And Richard White had said he would call. And before anyone knew it, the summer would be here again.

Mrs. Parker squeezed her daughter's hand. "Either I've been away a long time, or things change quickly," she said softly. "Because I don't have a little girl any longer. Miss Donna Parker is a young lady now."

Donna smiled shyly. "Could you really tell, Mommy? I *feel* so grown-up, but I didn't think it showed. I guess"— her face became quite serious—"I guess troubles have a way of aging a person."

It was so nice to have her parents back, so nice to have someone to—well, to lean on. On the other hand, it was wonderful to know that her parents realized, at last, that she was no longer a child.

"Do you think I'm grown-up enough to fly to California by myself this summer?" she asked. "You know, Uncle Roger invited me a long time ago, and I've never really been any place exciting. I've hardly been away from home at all, except for Grandma's, and Camp Cherrydale last summer, and they hardly count at all."

"If I know you, Cooky," said her mother, "you don't have to leave home to have excitement. The next two months will hold plenty of fun, I'm sure. And once school is over—about California—well, we'll see."

The ringing of the telephone brought Donna back sharply to the present.

"I'll answer it," she said gaily. With all her problems solved, surely the call could bring nothing but good news.

She hummed a little tune as she ran down the stairs toward the telephone call that would send her on a whole new set of adventures.

(Whitman)

Famous Classics

- Alice in Wonderland
- Fifty Famous Fairy Stories
- Little Men
- Robinson Crusoe
- Five Little Peppers and How They Grew
- Treasure Island
- The Wonderful Wizard of Oz
- The Three Musketeers
- Robin Hood
- Heidi
- Little Women
- Black Beauty
- Huckleberry Finn
- Tom Sawyer

Meet wonderful friends—in the books that are favorites—year after year

Fiction for Young People

THE RIFLEMAN
THE RESTLESS GUN
WAGON TRAIN
GENE AUTRY
The Ghost Riders
WYATT EARP
GUNSMOKE
ROY ROGERS
The Enchanted Canyon
DALE EVANS
Danger in Crooked Canyon
ROY ROGERS AND DALE EVANS
River of Peril
DRAGNET
BOBBSEY TWINS
Merry Days Indoors and Out
At the Seashore
In the Country
WALTON BOYS
Gold in the Snow
Rapids Ahead
ANNIE OAKLEY
Danger at Diablo
Double Trouble
NOAH CARR, YANKEE FIREBRAND
LEE BAIRD, SON OF DANGER
CIRCUS BOY
Under the Big Top
War on Wheels

HAVE GUN, WILL TRAVEL
MAVERICK
ASSIGNMENT IN SPACE
WITH RIP FOSTER
DONNA PARKER
At Cherrydale
Special Agent
On Her Own
TROY NESBIT'S
MYSTERY ADVENTURES
The Diamond Cave Mystery
Mystery at Rustlers' Fort
RED RYDER
Adventures at Chimney Rock
RIN TIN TIN
Rinty
Call to Danger
The Ghost Wagon Train
FURY
The Mystery at Trappers' Hole
LASSIE
Mystery at Blackberry Bog
The Secret of the Summer
Forbidden Valley
WALT DISNEY
Spin and Marty
Spin and Marty, Trouble at Triple-R
TRIXIE BELDEN
The Gatehouse Mystery
The Red Trailer Mystery
The Mystery off Glen Road
The Mysterious Visitor
Mystery in Arizona

(Whitman)

Adventure! Mystery! Read these exciting stories written especially for young readers

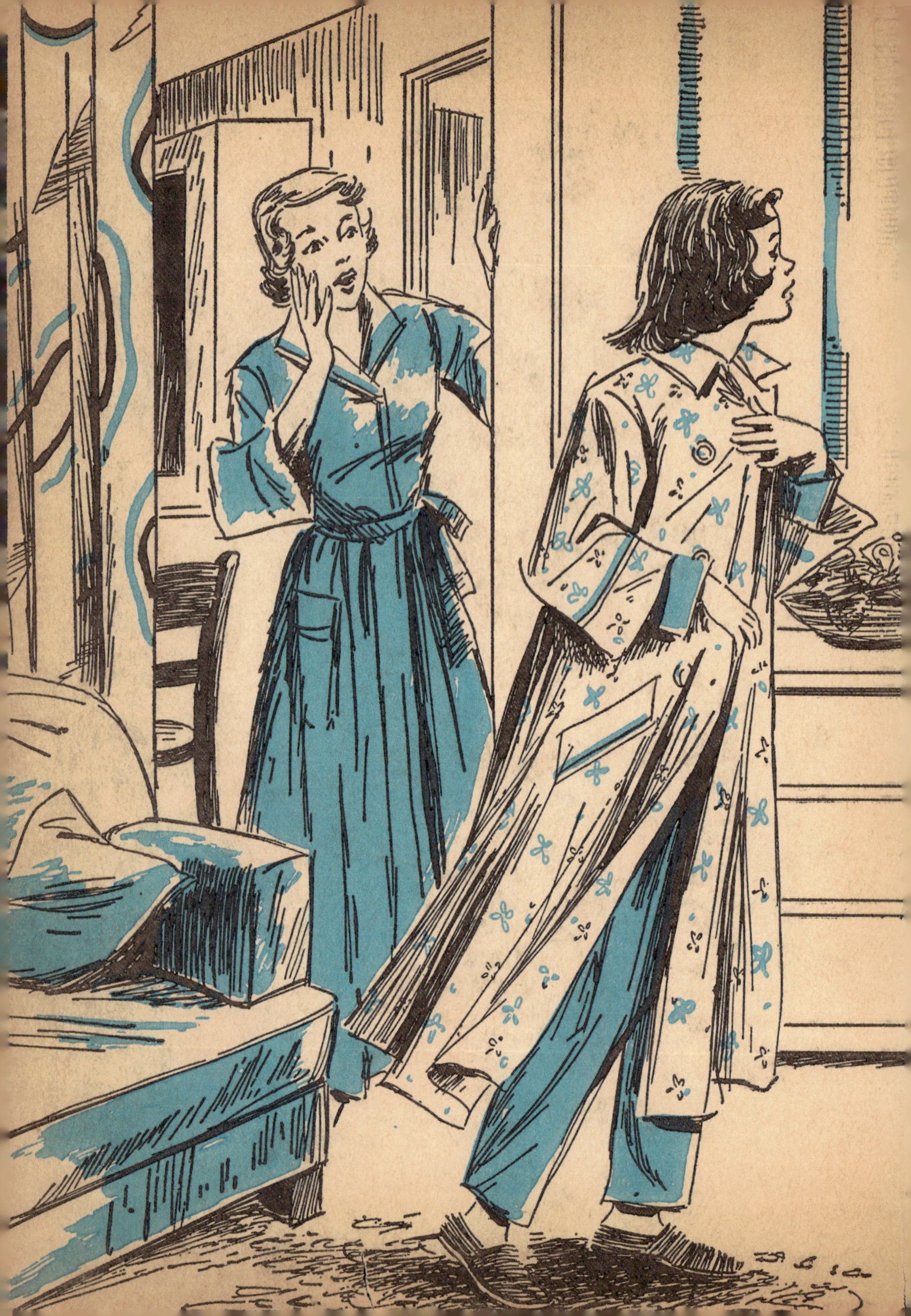